SEASON'S STRANGER

SEASON'S STRANGER

A NOVEL

WENDY BLACK FARLEY

Carpenter's Son Publishing

Season's Stranger

© 2017 by Wendy Black Farley

No part of this book may be reproduced or transmitted in any form or by any means, electronic or mechanical, including photocopying, recording, or by any information storage and retrieval system, without permission in writing from the copyright owner.

Published by Carpenter's Son Publishing, Franklin, Tennessee

Published in association with Larry Carpenter of Christian Book Services, LLC
www.christianbookservices.com

The ESV® Bible (The Holy Bible, English Standard Version®) copyright © 2001 by Crossway, a publishing ministry of Good News Publishers. ESV® Text Edition: 2011. The ESV® text has been reproduced in cooperation with and by permission of Good News Publishers. Unauthorized reproduction of this publication is prohibited. All rights reserved.

Edited by Robert Irvin

Cover Design by Debbie Manning Sheppard

Interior Layout Design by Suzanne Lawing

Printed in the United States of America

978-1-946889-11-9

All rights reserved.

seasonsstranger.com

This book is dedicated to mothers of special children. I know many and will not attempt to name them all. Their love and dedication are the closest representations of Jesus' love I have seen, and I believe this knowledge places them in a deeper understanding of the eventual rewards of Heaven.

Special thanks to Pamela Black Williams and Peggy Fuller for their unique talent for details.

CONTENTS

Gleaning and Gathering 11

Preparing for the Worst 19

A Work in Progress 31

A Different Kind of Gathering 37

Evade and Escape 49

The Underbelly 57

That's a Wrap! 67

Paranoid Much? 71

No Happy Hour Here! 78

Paranoid Much! 84

The Seduction 90

Deflated 99

Thankful 104

Need to Know 115

Without Words 121

Legal Eagles 129

"To the Church at Ephesus" 137

Connections—Old and New 143

Love Story 152

Frosted 162

Old Year's Resolution! 167

Privileged Information 172

Delivered 179

Dawn 184

The Informant 193

Very Merry 203

CHAPTER 1

GLEANING AND GATHERING

"Are you proud of yourself?"

It almost sounded like a reprimand. Ashton, the tech guy, wasn't the least concerned about gentle or indirect conversational styles, but Cori Sellers knew he meant well. Cori's thoughts were wrenched away from the stranger who was browsing through a display of plans for the annex to the town hall a few sections away from where she was finishing up for the day. Despite her fatigue mingled with daydreaming about the stranger, she struggled to form a contrasting, gentle response to Ashton.

"Well, Ashton, I am happy it seemed to go so well. Thanks for the save with the puppet play sound track."

"Yeah. It's my job."

"You're my rock!" Cori replied, once again in contrast to the absence of warmth coming from Ashton. Cori cared a great deal for him, but steadfastly stayed the course in attempting to model the subtle art of irony. Saying no more, and not picking up on the nuance of Cori's reply, Ashton smiled broadly while continuing to dismantle the speakers and wires he was preparing to remove from the premises.

Cori reflected on how she loved and understood Ashton and his directness. He occupied her thoughts for a moment as she realized someday he could meet someone who would thrill him to the core, dissolving his penchant for directness and allowing his many alluring traits to surface. She hated that it could be the perfect storm for when the initial glow wore off!

Suddenly her attention was drawn to a small commotion coming from the parking lot area. She heard someone shout, "Medic! Where's the medic? Quick!"

Cori immediately used her walkie-talkie to summon the medics, grabbed her friend, Jessalyn, who was a nurse—and nearby—and rushed to elbow her way through the crowd that was forming.

"Please, everyone, make a clearing for the medics and stand aside so help can get through." Cori repeated the request until the crowd had dispersed a bit and the nurse and medics were able to reach the victim, who seemed to be a young woman.

Cori quickly pulled her cell phone from her jacket and called an ambulance. A police officer who probably had been on the premises also arrived, and the stranger she had observed a moment before politely but forcefully had worked through the crowd that had quickly closed ranks again. The man knelt down with the medical team. She heard him call out, "Do you have Narcan?"

Cori knew what it meant, and she was aghast. There must be evidence of an overdose . . . but why would such a young woman, probably only a teen, have overdosed at a family event?

Quickly, a medic pulled items from his bag. She couldn't see what he was working with or exactly what he did, but before long there seemed to be movement on the part of the young woman.

Cori heard sirens and rushed out to the street to guide the ambulance as close to the scene as possible. Everyone and everything now became a blur. She felt herself white-knuckling her cell phone and forcing herself to relax her hand rather than crush the device. In a whir of activity, the young woman was on a stretcher and being wheeled to the ambulance. She caught a glimpse of what appeared to be the stranger entering the ambulance with the victim just before the doors closed and the vehicle wailed its way from the scene.

In her exhaustion, Cori's only wish was that the young woman would be OK. All her previous feelings for the day's event to be successful—and over—were now eclipsed by her concern for what had just happened.

Gleaning and Gathering was in its fifth year as a multi-organization service to the community of Laurel Ledge, where Cori lived. Churches, businesses, nonprofits, and residents of the Laurel Ledge area had a glorious time celebrating the fall season on the Saturday closest to Halloween. They were blessed with a beautiful day. The sun glowed its warmth through the bare trees and reflected off the thick carpet of fallen leaves strewn across the grounds. Whenever there was a break in the action at the food pantry where she volunteered, Cori drank in the vision of kids running around in their Halloween costumes, unable to resist throwing leaves at one another or over their heads, or pushing them together into a pile ready-made for cushioning their jumps and dives.

Cori also treasured an aspect of the event that was distinctive. Organizations provided folks with a variety of free services, information, and products. There were health screenings, food pantries, bounce houses, musical entertainment, farmers' markets, craft tables, demonstrations, pony rides, and an ever-increasing number of other fun activities. It was vintage New England, but, unlike the ubiquitous forms of harvest festivals that had sprung up around the northeast, this one was noncommercial. Almost none of the presenters charged for services or wares.

"Hey, nice work with the puppets!" Cori was wrenched from her stupor as she tried to process the kind words from an individual who had helped with the food pantry. "Try not to let the emergency detract from all of the good that happened today." The annual harvest event, which they abbreviated as The Gathering, was a huge undertaking. The gorgeous and unexpected warmth was giving way to a typical late-afternoon autumn chill. The words were warm and intended to comfort, but Cori was instead chilled and on edge.

She determined to remain engaged with participants in spite of her unsettled feelings. "You mean they weren't all staring up into space instead of facing the audience?"

"No. It was as though they could see us and were talking directly to us."

"I'm so glad to hear it. Controlling the hand puppets is trickier than it looks. If the puppet isn't staring up in the air, then the arm wand is forgotten or the mouth is gaping open as if catching flies! It's almost impossible for a novice to coordinate it all."

"Well, I'm in awe of your talent in training the young kids from your church youth group. Plus, the message, really, was clear. I could see the audience was getting it. Thanks for your patience in working with them. I'm just not that good with kids. And Cori, thanks for your tenacity in creating openings for presenting the gospel. It's just not in my wheelhouse."

Cori's heart was aching more than her feet, but she tried to be gracious to this very kind person. "Thank you, and everyone, for your many contributions to the day. I only have a small part to contribute."

Fatigued, Cori plodded through her share of the enormous take-down effort and then returned to her condo. She was desperate to hear how the teen was doing. Feet pounding and mind racing . . . and yet, just as desperately, she wished there was someone there to help her debrief and possibly rub her feet! Her thoughts slowed for the moment and drifted to the stranger who seemed to respond so promptly to the afternoon's medical emergency. He had caught her eye at various intervals during the afternoon as well. Admittedly, she didn't know everyone who attended the massive event, but she would love to know who this man was and enjoyed a few moments imagining what it would be like for him to be her foot masseur!

Cori suddenly felt guilty about her ridiculous daydreams. What was in her control was to talk to her brother. He always was available to listen and chat. Roman was Cori's adopted brother. Cori and Roman's parents were well along in years as they embarked on parenthood. By the time Roman was a senior in high school, both had passed away. Roman's chronic lung disease required ongoing treatments, though he currently was enjoying a measure of good health.

Cori worked hard even while being a full-time graduate student, helping him in any way she could, including aiding Roman in looking for a job. Over time it was not possible for him to maintain his health and full-time employment. Though Cori tried to keep close watch, and she wasn't aware of all the details from a human resources department point of view, ultimately, Roman was let go by his last employer. For years, Roman was supported by Cori.

Though Cori was as attentive as possible, even a sweet guy like Roman needed more than a sister. He became extremely depressed and lonely. Relationships were difficult for him, but he eventually met a wonderful girl online through a faith-based site. Ainsleigh, his love interest, also struggled with health issues, and lived in Arizona. A modest wedding in her home church, and a move there by Roman, took place the previous year.

Cori texted Roman that she wanted to talk, he called her immediately, and they chatted a long time, especially about the medical emergency.

Cori's habit of focusing on others had led to a near non-existent love life. Because she would admit her desires only to herself, she had no clue or advice on where to begin. She was aware that, unlike the heroines of the Christmas novellas she devoured during the holiday season, she wasn't "smoking hot," amazingly successful, or otherwise imbued with traits that would make her irresistible or even notable to many men. She was loving and giving, but she also had a penchant for justice that could be a deterrent to folks who would rather take a "don't-get-involved" approach to life.

Lacking the face-to-face dialogue she desired at that moment, Cori was left with pondering conversations that previously had taken place. . . . The thrill of seeing Della's obvious pleasure at The Gathering gave her a good feeling as she thought back to one of their many encounters during the day. Della was new to Cori's elementary-aged youth group from church.

"Aren't you exhausted?" Della's mom Reina had asked Cori as they arrived at the food pantry, where Cori worked in between the hourly puppet plays.

"Adrenalin is a wonderful thing!" Cori had responded, then turned to her daughter. "You are a natural with the puppets, Della. You have skills!" Cori locked in on Della's big brown eyes as they widened along with her smile, even while her shoulders came up and her head dropped a bit. Cori noted that Della seemed unaccustomed to praise and attention from an "influential" (to her) adult.

"Thank you." Della's reply was very soft . . .

. . . Cori's thoughts returned to the present. The loving relationship between Della and her mom Reina was heartening, but the sense that they had very little in the way of other comforts caused her heart to ache a bit as well. She disliked that Della's lifestyle difference—simply that she didn't have as many nice things—was noticed by the mostly middle-class youngsters in her youth group. Della seemed to thrive on the lessons and activities in the every-other-Monday night group. But there were few interactions with others in the group. Most of the children seemed far more inclined just to have a good time, and Cori often sensed an air of superiority over Della or any others who weren't part of the "core group."

An insensitive remark made by one of the youngsters often surfaced in Cori's memory—and made her cringe. The first time Della attended a meeting, one of the kids let this slip out: "Della goes to the rubber room at school."

Cori knew from experience with her brother that it meant nothing more than she received extra help at school. For Roman, it was necessary because of his absences that mounted throughout each school year. Cori often followed up insensitive remarks with gentle encounters. She had told that student: "We all need a little extra help now and then. Good thing for people smart enough to find it." . . .

. . . Again, her thoughts were interrupted. This time by Jessalyn's ringtone. Cori grabbed her cell and answered the call as quickly as she could.

"Jessalyn. How is everything? How is the girl?"

"Everything is going to be fine, Cori. She is doing better than I expected."

"Are you sure? Are you still at the hospital?"

"Yes. I wasn't going to leave until I knew all was well. The hospitalist has concluded from the medical tests that she is going to be fine. She really dodged a bullet. It's a good thing that Narcan was available on the scene."

"I'm so, so relieved. Thank the good Lord. I have so many questions. Do we know where she got the drugs? Do you know who the man is who recognized the need for Narcan?"

"I don't know who that guy is. I waited in the nurse's station for information and chatted with the staff while waiting. I don't know where he went. Whoever he was, this wasn't his first rodeo. I know that. What else did you ask?"

"Where did she get the drugs?"

"Oh yeah. The police have asked permission to question her, but that isn't a given under the circumstances. I think the family is considering it. I heard a rumor that a supplier was at the playground near the town common. It's sketchy, but nothing involving The Gathering. Please, this is not on you, Cori."

"I so hope not. Thanks, Jessalyn. I don't know what I would do without you. I also know you want to get home. Talk to you later."

Successful, thrilling, busy, exhausting—and a gorgeous day, weather-wise, thrown in. So why, despite such a great event, good memories, and the restored health of the teen girl, did Cori have these feelings of unease?

She was quite familiar with self-doubt, but this was different. Something was still amiss.

CHAPTER 2

Preparing for the Worst

Begrudgingly, Cori removed her sluggish frame from the sofa to get her cell on the kitchen island, where it remained after Jessalyn's update. Work was calling, and that was seldom a good thing on a weekend.

"Hello. It's Cori."

Sophie Gaston was the person on call at work this weekend.

"Hi, Cori. I came by The Gathering today for a bit. How are you holding up?" Cori was grateful that Sophie took time to attend, and it was quite politic of her to use what she knew was on Cori's mind as an entree to whatever bad news she was about to pass along.

"Oh thanks, Sophie. I'm resting, reflecting, and renewing! Did you hear what happened as The Gathering was winding down?" She filled in Sophie, who was appropriately concerned and shocked.

Coyly, Cori quickly added, "Also wondering what's up, Sophie?"

"Oh yeah. I know you must be exhausted, Cori. But I wanted to give you as much time to prepare for your next assignment as possible. The case involves a tragedy at a high school several hours from Laurel Ledge, and Amity Associates was called to put together a community crisis team for when the school resumes on Tuesday. It involves the suicide of a young man in the junior class of Snow Cliffs Valley Academy. I understand it to be somewhere near the Stowe region of Vermont."

"Oh wow, Sophie. I thought I was prepared for these calls. You've caught me a bit off guard." Cori worked as a counselor for Amity, an organization that provided support for individuals, groups, and communities in need of all sorts of assistance—somewhat beyond the services of a typical employee assistance program, though that was a big part of their business as well.

"I know, Cori. It took me several minutes after I first picked up the phone to actually call you. And that was before I knew about what you've just been through with the apparent overdose. If you're ready for this, Byron should work with you, and I'll leave it up to you to let him know. I'll write up the information and share the document with you on my document drive. As I think I said, school doesn't resume until Tuesday. I know you're tired, but at least there is an extra day to prepare." Sophie uttered the latter part rather sheepishly, almost as if there was a question mark at the end of the sentence.

Cori faltered a bit after her conversation with Sophie ended. Shoring up for an assignment like this was no easy task. There was so much to do, and she had to set aside her fatigue to move forward with the necessary initial steps. The first step was to let Byron know. Byron Camp was the coworker/counselor with whom she was paired most often. To her he represented both a colleague and friend. Whatever extra time they had spent on their friendship in the past was soon to come to an end. Byron and his wife were expecting a baby in a couple of months. She pondered for a moment how his life was about to change for a very long time, if not forever.

She quickly made the judgment that a text was an acceptable way to ease into informing him and Cheri that their weekend wouldn't be devoted exclusively to activities of their choice. *Sorry to say we caught a case. Call when you have a chance and we'll talk.* She never abbreviated or knowingly misspelled in her texts, even though she once read a book, titled *TTYL*, on the art of IM, aimed at middle school kids.

This message was enough for now. There would be the usual research and planning before arriving at the school, but she was comfortable giving Byron at least a few hours to respond before trying again.

Could this case be the source of her continued unsettled feelings? The unlikely explanation was dismissed as soon as it crossed her mind. Cori was a cautious person, perhaps even a worrier. Never would she see herself as a foreboder. It was something tangible, but why couldn't she identify what it was? Maybe the overdose victim wasn't as OK as Jessalyn was led to believe? Maybe The Gathering was the site where she had received the drugs? Was there another shoe to drop?

The hour was now late, and she found no energy reserves to initiate anything else. The thought of her neglected, dusty condo strewn with disparate artifacts unearthed in preparation for The Gathering bothered her. *No way I'm cleaning up now,* she thought with resolve. No way could she concentrate on research or even recreational reading. What else but the TV!

What she saw on TV was a slight lift to her mood. Despite the fact Halloween hadn't yet passed, Christmas images were beginning to appear on the TV screen through ads and the occasional Christmas programming. She endured with good humor the clanging complaints about "Christmas creep," because she loved rushing the season. If she could, she would make the Christmas season at least two months in full force—or maybe all year!

Her love for Christmas was in stark contrast to the views of her best friend, Simone, who was one of the biggest critics of Christmas traditions. Simone was the youth pastor at her church. Cori considered Simone to be enchanting—especially with youth. She could bring humor to nearly any situation. Even her criticism of Christmas and its "icons"—which was part of Simone's overarching admonition to people of faith on all things that smack of idols—was laced with hilarity. It wasn't a constant theme with Simone, and it certainly wasn't oppressive given the lilt she brought to any conversation.

That brought to mind the amazing Thanksgiving getaway Simone and her extended family planned each year. Sometimes as many as thirty-five or so folks gathered at the Briny Bluffs Resort in Maine for several nights, which included a hearty Thanksgiving dinner at a nice restaurant. Cori felt fortunate to have been included the past few years. She so looked forward to it.

For Cori, the getaway had turned into the formal beginning to her favorite time of year. The resort always was decorated for fall when they arrived. During the time of their stay it transformed into a Christmas wonderland. It was an amazing time to rest or walk the Marginal Way, be with people or enjoy a good book in solitude, swim or relax in either the indoor pool or indoor or outdoor hot tubs, go to movies in the hotel theater, or eat and eat some more! Cori gave out her first Christmas gifts of the season to any kids who attended. She also was known to throw in Christmas ties for the men and earrings for the ladies. She loved everything about it.

Her immediate reverie led to the thought, *Why haven't I heard from Simone about the reservations since they typically need to be made by now?* Simone. She had enough energy left to reach out to Simone. The only question was should she text or call? She hadn't seen that much of Simone at The Gathering, and when she had, they didn't seem to have time to say even a few words to each other. Come to think of it, it seemed a little tense between them. She decided on a text.

Hey Simone. Are you as tired as I am? The teen praise band was great. Usually Simone got right back to her, but there was no response. Cori could surmise that she was preoccupied given the day and the season. Cori decided to go to bed.

Mercifully, she slept the entire night—and yet, restlessly.

Byron called just as she was about to leave for church the next morning.

"Hey Byron."

"Hey. Cheri and I caught dinner and a late show last night, so my ringer was off. By the time I noticed your text, I waited rather than take a chance on disturbing you. I'm sure you needed your rest. How did it go, by the way?"

"Oh, everything went really well until the event was over." She proceeded to tell Bryon the story of the waning minutes on site at The Gathering. "And you're right, I was pretty out of it last night. Thanks for the thought! How was the movie?" She was about to punch serious holes in what was left of Byron's weekend and possibly his week, so she wanted to be as nice as possible about it.

She then filled him in on what little she knew. "Would you be able to meet for a lunch and some planning time at the Sandwich Club?"

"Sure. Are you going to church?"

"Yeah. I'd better get going. Will one o'clock work for you?"

"Yup. That's fine."

After she shared the file with Byron's document drive, Cori recognized she would be late to church.

Attendance seemed excellent as evidenced by the difficulty she had in finding a parking place. No matter. The church was on the town square where The Gathering had taken place the day before, so there was ample parking. She had to walk a bit of distance, but Cori was fine with that.

She slid into the back of the church as unnoticed as she could. The two hundred-seat auditorium was comfortably full, and the enthusiastic congregation was in full swing with the same youth band that had performed the day before. Simone was up front in the thick of things.

It was a long service. More and more, the church Advisory seemed to be adding events to the service, and it irked Cori more than a little. Lively discussions about the pros and cons of the prolonged service had taken place between Simone and Cori; Simone pro and Cori con, surprisingly. Cori expected Simone to opine on the many aspects of the service represented by religious icons in the same way she always did with Christmas icons. Not so.

Perhaps it was the vestiges of fatigue impacting Cori's mood, but she was a little hurt that no mention of The Gathering was included in the church bulletin, even though she had prepared a small note thanking everyone who had a part. As the initiator and coordinator of the event, her heart swelled with gratefulness for the many folks who made it all work. She knew her part paled in comparison to the collective talents of everyone involved. Cori needed no praise, and she was embarrassed when anyone mentioned her efforts, but she also knew that a word of acknowledgement to those involved goes a long way.

What bothered her more was the chronic differential treatment of people. Particular congregants routinely received public praise for even the silliest efforts. This wasn't putting her in the right spirit for worship, and she tried to shake the feelings of this particular slight.

Cori felt rushed to meet with Byron by the time the service ended. The two events nearly overlapped, so Cori didn't have a chance to connect with folks at the coffee fellowship. She took the time to approach Simone, but never caught her eye. Cori left with a more intense feeling of unease than she had felt the day before. Her thoughts migrated from *Is something up?* to *What's up?*

Laurel Ledge never had the exclusive coffee shop or cupcake bakery so present in other towns where folks seemed to pair off or meet for quick chats. But it was fortunate to have the Sandwich Club, which specialized in sandwich branding. Even better, the store had all the specialty coffees, teas, cupcakes, and pies that made some individual stores such a big deal. It had designer soups in season as well. For Cori, one of the hallmarks of the store was the variety of chicken sandwiches that were paired with various flavors of chutney.

Byron was waiting for her when she arrived. He had chosen a seat close to the fireplace, which was built with stone resembling ledge festooned with lighted garlands of laurel. It was corny and surprisingly chic at the same time.

Cori greeted him and went to order her seasonal pumpkin soup and Puducherry Pocket—chicken salad made with Indian-spiced chutney. When she sat down, she launched into a rant.

"I'm so sorry I'm late. Singing and a sermon. Who needs anything more when people of faith get together? Announcements were first and went on and on. Then there has to be recruiting for events, the covered dish brigade reminding of the upcoming dinner, the moderator having to add some homey story about his latest family trip, a random announcement or comment 'from the floor,' the choir, singing, a forty-five-minute sermon, more singing to make sure the songs sum up the forty-five-minute sermon . . . " Cori stopped to catch her breath. Byron was silent. Cori felt guilty. "Sorry. You've heard it all before. I hate to make excuses, but I guess I'm on overload right now. I needed church to be comfort—not to create more of a strain."

Byron smiled. "I'm giving you a hard time." He wasn't a frequent attender of church.

"No, really. I am sorry. Not a good way to start our work. But I really am a bit upset that I've done something to offend Simone. For the life of me, I can't think of what I might have done."

Byron didn't respond this time, but she was left feeling awkward and sensing that Byron had an opinion yet to be expressed.

She was gathering the written information she had received from Sophie when, suddenly, she noticed the stranger who had responded to the emergency with the overdose victim the day before. He glanced over at her, and their eyes locked—this was much more than a glance. Her eyes might have seized up for the moment, but her heart hadn't! She feared her breathing would start mimicking the pounding of her heart. For a moment, it was as though he knew she envisioned his hands comforting her sore feet. He smiled and, having paid his tab, turned and left. She felt the blood drain from her face. The most salient feeling from his gaze was that it was delicious. Why hadn't she jumped to her feet and asked him about yesterday? She could be so witless at times—seemingly when it was of utmost importance to keep her wits about her.

It all happened in a microsecond, but Byron noticed. "Someone you know?"

She cleared her throat, afraid she had no voice at all. "Oh, no. But I noticed him at The Gathering yesterday."

"I'd say you noticed." His voice cracked slightly, as men's voices often do when they're teasing. "So, someone you would like to know?"

"Silly. He's the one who saved that girl's life yesterday. I don't know why I didn't jump up when I saw him, introduce myself, and thank him. That's all. Let's get to work."

"OK. But I think there's a lot more than you just wanting to thank him!" Cori didn't respond to Byron; instead, she kept fiddling with the paperwork she had brought for their meeting.

Byron finally realized he should return to the task. "I brought the outline we usually follow to make sure we've covered everything." They had worked on numerous community emergencies, so they developed a template that made planning, arduous though it may be, flow fairly well. However, it wasn't common for them to deal with the suicide of a young person. "I guess we should be thankful we don't have a lot of experience with this scenario, even if it will cause us more work." Aloud, Byron had mirrored her thoughts.

"For sure it will add some layers of complexity since we'll be working with a bunch of grieving young people as well as adults. I'll access the American Psychological Association website to check on the latest statistics regarding teen self-harm and suicide—especially lethality. I could use a refresher on best practices when responding to the needs of the age groups we'll be dealing with—if I can find it. Oh, and I'll call the police department to see if I can get the police report faxed to my home."

"Yeah, good. I think I'll call the school's executive director to find out more about the school. It would be helpful to get his take on the school's culture and how they might react in this situation." He thought for a moment and added, "As if he can really know that. I guess I meant whether they're typically a reactive student body. I'd also like to know what programs they offer on bystander reporting of bullying and other potential high-risk behaviors. Sometimes it's part of a mandatory health program. He should know if the school has been through crises of any sort before, and also if they had any indication this student was acting out in any way that would have hinted at suicide or ideation. Luckily, Sophie gave us a lot of cell phone numbers. That'll make it easier to get started."

After more than an hour of planning and chatting, Cori and Byron decided to wrap up and get started with their individual tasks.

"How is Cheri feeling?" Cori had been intending to ask sooner about the progress of Cheri's pregnancy. "I'm far more curious than the frequency of my questions would imply. I'm sorry for that. Really."

"She's doing fine. She's reaching out to others who have been through it, and she's beginning to 'get' how lucky she is to feel so well. She is a little chagrined, shall we say, about the weight gain. According to her, the doctor thinks she's weighing in a little heavier than he would prefer."

Cori laughed. "Wouldn't we all love to have as good an excuse as she has in that regard? Say hi to her for me, and please apologize for the time this is taking away from your weekend."

"Will do. Take care. Text or call when you have something I need to know."

Cori ventured to drive by Simone's apartment before returning home. It wasn't unusual to drop in on one another as each considered the other's place their home away from home. Simone's Avalanche wasn't in the drive, however, so Cori drove on.

Sometimes it suited Cori to get her outer world organized before embarking on an uncharted task, such as preparing for Tuesday morning at Snow Cliffs Valley Academy. So she hummed some show tunes while tidying up her house and vacuuming. She was relieved that her energy was somewhat restored.

She also needed a workout, but realized it was too late in the day. She was a member of the local YMCA, which she preferred over the many local gym options, mostly because of the standing Ys have in each community—not to mention the pool! For Cori, a workout was free weights combined with either the elliptical or swimming.

Now she needed her attention to return to the case. As agreed, she called the police department in the locale where they would be working to ask about the police report; the right officials agreed to fax it to her home. She felt relief that she wouldn't have to wait for it or drive several hours to retrieve it.

She connected with Byron again after reading the report. "The police report is pretty straightforward, at least after an initial read. I'll look at it more closely later on."

Byron said his talk with the executive director didn't produce any information that would send them in a direction other than what they had planned—except for one thing. "He mentioned that the faculty are in school all day tomorrow with in-service activities. He suggested that we arrive tomorrow to meet with them in the afternoon. Why don't you call the school counselor for the deceased? I think it would give you a feel for the school, and he would be the best guy for helping us connect with the major players when we arrive on the scene. I imagine he knew the deceased, Anderson."

Each provided updates on their research to one another and emailed summaries to follow up.

Cori was about to dial the cell of the school counselor when she decided to call Simone instead. Wherever Simone had been, she guessed there was plenty of time for her to arrive home by now. She called the landline so she wouldn't be invasive, just in case. Cori was surprised when Simone picked up.

It was a pretty hollow "Hello." Occasionally, Cori surprised herself by responding normally in a somewhat abnormal situation. Sometimes that was good; sometimes it felt like denial.

"Hey, Simone. Seems like it's been too busy to talk. How's it going?" Simone was still cold. "It's OK." No follow-up. Cori knew things were far from OK between them, but still tried to be cool about it.

"So, usually by now we've made our reservations at the Briny Bluffs Resort for Thanksgiving. I realized I hadn't gotten the prompt from you yet. Should I go ahead and call?"

There was quite a pause, and then Simone said, "I don't think we're going this year."

Without thinking, Cori asked, "Why not?"

"Well, I think it's run its course." Simone sounded so deadpan. Not only did her tone make no sense, neither did her assertion that the holiday gathering had run its course. There was only a split-second for those thoughts, and Simone added, "Listen, Cori, I have to go." Click.

It started to make sense why things made no sense. Something was up, and she wasn't willing to admit it to herself during The Gathering. She hadn't wanted the day marred by uncomfortable thoughts, so she suppressed the behavior she now realized was more than mere suspicion regarding Simone. Her mind quickly identified myriad ways in which Simone had snubbed her the day before. She had to find out what was wrong.

CHAPTER 3

A WORK IN PROGRESS

Cori was stunned. She had finally gotten through to Simone, but she really hadn't. Her only realization was that she knew less of what was going on than before. What had she done now? Cori wanted to curl up in a ball and stay there. But she didn't have time for that. She shouldn't have been distracted from her work, and she needed to initiate contact with the school counselor. It could take a few attempts before they would have a live conversation, so she decided to try before the hour was too late.

She reached him on the second ring. "Hello. This is Paul Westrock."

"Hello. My name is Cori Sellers. I've been told about the tragic loss of one of your students. I work with a man named Byron at Amity Associates, and together we want to provide any assistance we can to you and the school community in the upcoming days. Please know, first of all, that we care very much about what you're going through."

"Thank you. It's good to know we'll have help. I'm sure we'll need it. What can I do to help you?"

"You know the community best. Hearing anything that you think is salient would be helpful."

He seemed young and easy to talk with. "Well, I need to be honest about being new to the school, but I think I knew Anderson quite well. I intentionally jumped in during the fall to work with the junior class on large-group—mostly classroom—activities. It's a good time to begin hands-on college planning."

He hesitated a bit, cleared his throat, and continued with a slight hitch in his voice. "Anderson was a spirited guy. He drew attention to himself no matter where he was. He had a lot of questions, so I spent time with him in my office one on one as well. I think it was a ruse to get out of class, but that's no matter. It was good to have the time to make connections with him."

There was another pause, then he continued. "I think I can anticipate a question you'll need to have answered. He never hinted at any self-harm, nor did I notice any cutting or anything. I had a few reports of that kind of behavior with regard to other students, but never Anderson. This is an absolute shock to me."

Cori thought she knew the exact type of kid Westrock was talking about. *Spirited.* That was code for a student known for classroom behaviors that could, at times, be distracting to the educational process. Perhaps even most of the time. She didn't press Westrock for particulars; obviously, he was shaken by the death and understandably wished to speak as well of Anderson as possible.

They both knew she needn't be privy to a play by play on details of his classroom behaviors since she was only interested in how to help Westrock and his students. Shock was an obvious reaction, but it went beyond that for Westrock, who repeated his surprise.

"Anderson was part of a pretty entitled group of kids. He was a skier, and that's a big deal in this area, as you can imagine." He was referring to the proximity to the Stowe area and its opportunities for skiing. He continued. "Most of the members of the team enjoyed the notoriety, including Anderson. He seemed comfortable in his own skin, as well as in the school and community environments. Really, I missed this completely."

Cori tried to reassure him. "Please don't feel this is on you in any way. I've read the police report, and there was no indication to anyone that there was a history of self-harm. His parents reported much the same information on his demeanor to the police. It is obvious you will be an integral part of the team we will form as we work with the school community. If I come up with other questions, is this a good number to call?"

"Yes. Please. If there is anything I can do, please don't hesitate to ask. I can't seem to focus on anything else right now."

"Thanks. If you don't hear from me, I look forward to meeting you tomorrow."

As the call ended, Cori thought about how perfect this man seemed for his job. He seemed to have the patient openness that engenders the trust needed for reciprocation. Most of all, he seemed prepared to be in it for the long haul—which, in high school, is a minimum of a four-year period. Cori imagined that whether a student was shy, acting out, or a combination of both, Westrock was a patient listener and problem-solver. Cori admired and envied that kind of counselor. She had faced reality, some time ago, that she was not that person. She had landed the perfect job for a counselor who was short-term and solution-oriented.

Cori reread the police report just to double-check her

notion that comments from Anderson's family referenced no prior suicide attempts. She had genuinely tried to console Westrock and didn't believe he should feel guilty. But Cori had been around long enough to establish her own value system, and it might have been a bit on the jaded side. She considered just about anything that was dangerous as self-harm when it came to young people: sex, alcohol, drugs, cutting, hairpulling, anorexia, bulimia—perhaps there was no way to make an exhaustive list. In her opinion, a family, or counselor, might know very little about the activities of an adolescent except overt suicide attempts. The police report said nothing of scars on other parts of the body, just the obvious injury to the neck resulting from the method used by Anderson to take his life. She couldn't help but question to herself: *Are all scars visible?*

She called the police department again and identified herself with the desk officer. "Thanks so much for getting the report on the suicide to me so quickly. I was wondering if I also could access the autopsy?"

"Ah, autopsies take a while, and the reports take even longer. Probably well into week after next."

Cori thanked him again and realized she and Byron would have finished their work in the area by the time the autopsy was produced, so the remainder of Cori's information for the near future would be what they could elicit from the clients she, Byron, Westrock, and other supporting members of the community were able to bring forward.

So much of Cori's time was spent traveling that she kept some luggage ready to go with an accompanying list of suggestions for various staples. Typically, she opted for a safe wardrobe of pantsuits, suits, or a skirt, blouse, and sweater. She added jeans this time. If she dared wear them, they might make her more presentable to a student population—if the school allowed jeans.

Cori was weary and looked forward to rest. But she

dreaded bedtime. Seldom could she fall asleep promptly. She feared she would be interviewing students in her sleep. She wasn't a dream therapist and had no idea why she relived or previewed her life in such bizarre ways while sleeping. A little rest, though, she knew, would be so welcome. She wanted to call Simone, but it was too late, so she resisted.

Cori was dreaming about the television program she was watching when she was startled by the telephone. She had dozed off while playing back one of the Christmas movies previously set to record on the DVR. Though disoriented, it didn't take long for her to grab the phone without checking the caller ID.

"Hello." In her drowsiness, she found herself fumbling with the phone.

"Cori, we need to talk." It was Simone. "You've got to apologize to Eugenia about the way you've been treating Mason and Gil."

Eugenia was the mom of Mason and Gil, two of the youngsters in Cori's youth group. Eugenia also was director of communications at Cori's church and the presumed leader of just about everything else, in Cori's opinion. Mason and Gil were—in the same words as used by Westrock—spirited. They talked incessantly and had plenty of energy for anything—as long as it didn't involve being helpful. But for the most part, Cori kept those impressions to herself, with the exception of some venting to Simone.

Cori emerged from her sleepiness as quickly as she could. "What is up, Simone?"

Simone, in carefully measured words and a tone actually quite frightening to Cori, said, "It's about your yelling at them and telling them they didn't know anything about puppets. Eugenia is furious. You told them they always act awful, and no way would you let them touch the puppets. And what's all this fawning over the new kid, Della?"

Cori's mind was reeling from both the attack from Simone and the misinformation. Neither had more than a shred of basis in reality! Where was the support Simone always entrusted to Cori? Each knew the care the other displayed in working with her respective youth group. To be sure, Cori would freely admit she wasn't as charmed as Simone in her relationships. But there always was an understanding between them of how unjustly critical parents could be. Cori was quite sure Simone knew Eugenia to be a doting mom who viewed her sons as if they were the brightest and most well-behaved of their generation.

Anger and impatience with the obvious blindside were rising in Cori. At this point in her thoughts, Cori blurted out, "They didn't show up for the rehearsals, for corn sake! I didn't say those things anyway." Anger gripped her. "Don't be such a suck-up, Simone. And don't pretend to be as clueless as Eugenia."

Silence. Disconnect. Simone had hung up, leaving no opportunity for follow-up, clarification, or discussion.

CHAPTER 4

A DIFFERENT KIND OF GATHERING

Cori was still reeling from Simone's attack—or, her attack on Simone—but the drive through Vermont the next morning brought some renewal. She loved Vermont. Crossing the border provided an instant reminder that one had arrived in beautiful surroundings. From the rolling mountains to the immediate thinning of traffic, one was aware that everything had changed. There was no clear explanation for why the hills and valleys provided so much for her to drink in, but they always worked for Cori. She hadn't spent long periods of time there, but an overnight typically was all she needed to feel refreshed and ready for reentry into her world. Her current mood was much improved, and she felt ready to face the crisis at hand.

Byron and Cori intended to follow through with the suggestion to get together with as many faculty and staff from the school as possible on this Halloween afternoon. "I think it's genius that the executive director has an in-service for faculty on a day when kids are unlikely to be able to concentrate." She had expressed this opinion to Byron on their way through Vermont.

They departed early in the morning and arrived in time for coffee at the Purple Polka Dot diner near the school. They were thankful to be able to check in early at the hotel and prepare themselves for the first meeting of what would be a daunting series of days.

During coffee, though trying to resist her selfish impulse to vent, Cori gave in to her hurt and told Byron about her conversation with Simone. Maybe they were both tense, maybe Byron was sick of her venting, or maybe he simply thought Cori's whining was ill-timed, but he responded in a way Cori had never experienced from him before. She was stunned, and all she gleaned from his terse response was, "I'm sorry, Cori, but what did you really expect?"

They paid the bill and left in silence. For the second time in a twelve-hour period, Cori was stunned.

Westrock greeted them warmly as they entered the school. They had texted him a few minutes before their arrival.

"Welcome to Snow Cliffs Valley. I'm sad to introduce you to the school under these circumstances. It really is a special place, except right now. How about a quick tour while we wait for the faculty meeting to take a break?"

To Cori, it was a relief to meet Westrock. She felt some levity amid the dark thoughts she was struggling with. This came almost singularly through the fact that just about any woman with a pulse would like to meet this fine man. Not "beefcake" fine. In fact, she wondered whether he aspired to identify as metrosexual; his clothing style fell just a tad short of convincing Cori one way or the other.

Cori knew just how ridiculous these wanderings of her mind were; she wouldn't voice these thoughts to anyone. Speaking of looks, she was surprised by her first glimpse of the school's executive director, who was emerging from the faculty meeting that was breaking up. Folks were filing out into the hallway for a break. She gave Byron a side glance and whispered, "I knew it was ridiculous to have pictured the headmaster from *Gilmore Girls*. But I wasn't even close. This man seems more like the hot English teacher from that show."

Byron merely made an unapproving grimace in response. *OK*, Cori told herself. *Enough of the scenery. You need to focus on the mission here.*

The executive director, Walter Langston, approached and shook their hands.

"Thank you both for coming, and for responding so quickly. We'll meet with the faculty right after this quick break."

When the faculty regrouped, Cori and Byron were introduced and spent some time learning the names and roles of as many folks as possible. It wasn't a huge school, but there were at least fifty faculty members present.

They listened to general anecdotes about Anderson, the deceased teen, outlined the protocols that would be in place, and answered questions about the process.

Bryon finished their first presentation. "What's most important is taking care of yourselves first. Listening to the needs of the students is important, but it will only work if you're doing OK."

Langston added one item of information. "Please be sure any students who leave your classroom sign out as always. We always need to know where students are, but it is even more important under these circumstances."

Cori and Byron fielded questions and comments from the floor. Anyone who wished to stay for the smaller groups that followed were encouraged to do so. It seemed that most stayed.

Cori teamed with the executive director in one group. Bryon teamed with the dean of students; Westrock, along with the other school counselor, also met with a group. Though grieving themselves, it was apparent to Cori and Byron that many of these staff members were centered and would be most helpful in the days ahead.

Cori observed a small group of faculty members, however, that left instead of joining a group. She watched and noted that this group seemed cohesive and didn't exit the building. Cori certainly didn't know all the names and roles at this point, but she was quite sure the school's athletic director was the decided leader of this group. She filed away the faces so she could follow up in some way.

"Wow. That was rather intense," Byron said to Cori a bit later. Byron was referring not only to the time it had taken them to speak with the full-time faculty, but also the time spent preparing guest teachers for possible roles they would be playing in the days ahead. "Let's get some dinner. I'm starved and desperately in need of a break."

"I'm glad our first day didn't start until early afternoon," Cori answered.

Byron agreed. "Right. I think it's a good group."

"Yeah. But I can't help but be tense about this whole thing."

Dinner with Byron was somewhat focused on the eating, but it was mostly about evaluating plans and reflecting on how they had been accepted by the school faculty.

"I think we're as prepared as we can be for the return of students to the building," Byron, always the optimist, said.

"Yeah, well, I sense they're a really concerned group of

people," Cori said. "I'm glad the executive director went along with our suggestion of guest teachers. Even if no one uses them, it's just the idea that no adult is stuck in front of a group of adolescents if a wash of grief floods their thoughts." She paused, remembering something else. "I can't help but wonder about what looked like a splinter group. Did you see them?"

Byron nodded. "My take on them was they needed time to process together. They're probably a clique, yes. But that's nothing new. There will always be some detractors when it comes to outsiders. You know that."

"I wish I wasn't so suspicious. Thanks. I just couldn't summon up good scenarios for their separating from the groups other than if they wanted to go home. Which they didn't."

Her thoughts shifted to another group they hadn't met. "Do you think it's a good idea to talk to the police?"

"For what reason?" Bryon looked really puzzled.

"I don't really know." Cori looked equally puzzled, but for different reasons.

"Was there something in the report I missed?" Byron was always the analytical one, and his question seemed an appropriate one.

"Not really. The report itself indicated little doubt as to what took place. But was it a little too pat and too well-written?" Cori, always the intuitive one. She was a prolific reader of things not written.

"It didn't strike me that way."

"Well, I'm jealous of your trust."

"Cori, what's not to trust? You're not making any sense. But you're going there anyway, aren't you?"

"Yeah. But you don't have to come."

"Yes. I know. It's your pursuit. But I'll come." That was Byron. Almost all the time he was the consummate gentleman. Byron was somewhat older than Cori, and if he hadn't been married, she acknowledged to herself a long time ago, she would have fallen hard for him. She wouldn't mind meeting someone with his looks and temperament. The former weren't perfect, but they were good enough. The latter, better than could be expected in most relationships. Would she ever have a relationship? Shouldn't she be content with being independent and single?

* * * * *

The desk officer, naturally, was the first person they encountered inside the police station.

"Hey," Cori began. "We probably have talked on the telephone. I'm Cori Sellers, and this is Byron Camp. We're here to consult with faculty and students at Snow Cliffs Valley Academy about the recent suicide. We were wondering if we could speak to the investigating officer."

"Probably you remember that the chief wrote the report," the officer said. "He volunteered to join the investigation and did the write-up, even though he wasn't on duty at the time the body was discovered. He's here, but he might not have time to talk with you. Have a seat, and I'll check."

Chief Joel Barrett soon appeared, and he proved professional and welcoming as he invited them into his office. "I'm glad you folks are here to help. I'm guessing there are some painful days ahead for the folks in this community."

Cori did the only questioning; Byron listened. "Chief, why did you volunteer to investigate and write the report even though an experienced detective was the first one on the scene?"

The chief didn't show any annoyance with her question. "This is a big deal in such a small community. I just thought the highest rank possible should take responsibility."

Cori didn't show any annoyance at his answer; she continued. "The report says there were no indications Anderson was a suicide risk. Did you probe that angle and try to determine if there was any other explanation for his death?"

Byron shifted. She was going to hear about this line of questioning later.

Barrett was nonplussed. "There was no evidence to prompt a further investigation."

Cori wasn't giving up. "If the autopsy report suggests otherwise, are you willing to consider other explanations for his death?"

"Ah, sure. Of course. But I'm not expecting anything different. We'll know soon." To Cori, Barrett seemed to be giving the situation the brush-off in spite of the big deal he said it was for the community. Cori noted with interest that he still showed no annoyance at her questions.

Cori expected to be rebuked on the drive to their hotel, albeit gently, for her treatment of the chief on the drive home. But Byron didn't address the conversation at all. He simply said, "Do I need some sleep."

In the end, Cori thought the interview easily could have been skipped—except for the information that it *didn't* provide. At least that was Cori's private thought, and even she wasn't sure what the chief's reactions meant.

Amazingly, Cori slept. Perhaps it was the amazing hotel room. It was a small establishment, but the rooms were spacious and had the best furnishings. The décor was very colonial, something she hadn't previously encountered in her travels. There were no less than six pillows standing up and overlapping on her king-size bed. The pillows were the best she had found, and she was sure they were made of down. She had never considered buying products made with down; perhaps she should reconsider.

* * * * *

Morning arrived, and Cori and Byron were swept away in a flurry of interviews and group meetings. They had written a script that would be read by all the first-block classes.

Dear Students, Faculty, and Staff,

A shared sadness over the death of a member of our community is an ever-present reality in our school today. Anyone among us may need to pause from the daily routine to grieve and continue to process the thoughts and feelings we have about the loss of Anderson.

Faculty and staff may call the office for the assistance of guest teachers. Students may obtain passes at any time, no matter how often it is necessary, to leave the classroom environment for designated areas to obtain help and support. Only names and destinations will be recorded; information shared is subject to the same confidentiality provided in any counselor setting.

Thank you for your presence today. Together, we can support each other and promote the educational process to the extent possible given our sense of loss.

At the end of the day, Byron and Cori debriefed one another before their scheduled meeting with the administration and school counselors. Alone, they began checking their records.

"Byron, very few if any of Anderson's closest friends responded to me for assistance," Cori told him. "Admittedly, girls are more apt to access these kinds of services, but in spite of the fact that several girls were listed as possible points of contact, none of them came to me. How about you?"

Byron checked his notes and compared them to the list he and Cori had received. "Nope. Nothing on my end either."

Cori didn't want to dominate the conversation when they were joined by the administration, but she couldn't contain her worries.

"Mr. Langston, Byron and I both noted the lack of interest

in support from Anderson's identified list of friends."

"Yes, Cori," Langston began. "We're not oblivious to that fact. Each classroom had a sign-out list of students who left the respective classrooms. I agree to check the sign-out records to determine who among them was in school and, if so, whether they simply remained in classes."

Cori was thankful they were willing to check on this, but she decided to be even more proactive. She dropped by the main office on her way out of school to have a chat with the real bosses—the administrative assistants.

"Hi. We met yesterday. I'm Cori," she said to the two women behind the counter.

One of the two answered. "Yes. We remember. I hope all went OK. Can we help you with something?" The other woman nodded.

"Well, first, I wanted to let you know I realize you are the ones who really run the school."

Both chuckled. Neither doubted her sincerity, nor the fact she was joking with them at the same time.

They also knew she wanted something.

"I think some of the students need a little encouragement to seek our help, but I'm not sure how to reach them."

The second woman responded in a way that gave Cori assurance they were willing allies. "We deliver passes to first-block classes for students with whom counselors or administrators wish to conference. Would you like some of the passes?"

"I would. But how do I find out the locations of their first-block classes?"

"We wouldn't mind filling out that part of the passes." The first woman came back to the conversation. Cori thought she might have perceived a wink from this woman. These women were a hoot. She wished she had met them under different circumstances.

Cori filled out the passes for the names of the students she wished to see and for the room she would use, then left them for the "bosses" to finish and deliver.

"Thanks so much. See you both tomorrow." Cori, in fact, did deliver a wink to the two women.

School released at 2:30, but Cori and Byron didn't return to their hotel until well after 5 p.m. They refreshed and went for dinner at a cute Thai restaurant. Cautious that folks were becoming more aware of them and their purpose in the community, they avoided any discussion of the case while they enjoyed a delicious meal of Khao Pad and Kai Med Ma Muong.

The conversation and mood seemed so normal between them that Cori decided not to confront Byron's comment, early in this trip, about Simone and their relationship. But clearly, it was on her mind. Instead, they had a lively discussion about the town, the tourist attractions in the area, and how some day they would like to return under different circumstances. She told Byron she had once visited the nearby skiing attraction of Stowe.

"OK. I know you like to snowshoe, but I didn't know you were a skier," Byron commented with a chuckle.

"Well, I convinced one of my friends to come with me to tour the HGTV dream home of 2011, which is less than an hour from here."

Byron chuckled again. Then laughed out loud. "Why on earth . . . ?"

"I knew you would scoff. Come on, you know how I love that kind of thing. I entered to win two times a day during the entire entry period. I actually hoped I would have a chance until I saw the bins and bins and warehouses of entries. I haven't lost interest in dreamy home decor, but I don't register to win anymore. Well, maybe my interest is waning a bit—I missed the White House Christmas decoration tour last year. That's a first!"

He couldn't help laughing again. "So, there are numerous

artisans, gift shops, and all sorts of other sightseeing in the area. Did you do any of that?"

"Not much."

Again, Byron laughed, pretty much openly and out loud.

Cori turned much more serious. "I wonder if we will associate this area with this tragedy forever," she said, her demeanor quieter.

"Probably."

Dinner was a reprieve from the pressure of work as well as the situation with her best friend. As soon as Cori was alone in her room, however, her heavy heart returned, and she realized that as much as she dreaded the thought, she was on the verge of a crying jag. Maybe that was good. It was quite typical of her to suppress sadness and worry; she had done so many times during Roman's numerous emergencies and the deaths of her parents. But she hated recovering from crying, so she tried to think of anything that would divert her attention.

Cori realized that during the chaos of the days—actually, weeks—leading to The Gathering, there were many times she had neglected her daily Bible reading and reflection. She had brought with her on this trip a study in the book of Proverbs. In this moment, Cori decided she had run out of excuses for her much-needed study. This was such a conflict in her life. She derived a refreshing when she began the day with the reminders of love and grace she encountered with every devotional reading, but the discipline to stay faithful with her Bible reading was a lifelong struggle.

The particular reading she picked up that evening centered on the definition of a fool. One thing that struck Cori was that a fool vents her feelings. That statement hit home for her. "Ouch," she heard herself saying, out loud. No matter what Byron had meant by his comment—"What did you really expect?"—she felt shame that she had vented to him so often. He wasn't part of her congregation and only knew what she shared with him. Typically, it was the bad things. Gossip also was determined as the mark of a fool, the Proverbs taught. "Ouch again!" Cori heard herself saying.

Was it torture rather than comfort she was receiving from this particular portion of her study? After some reflection, however, she realized all of it was helping steer her attitude away from wallowing in her own problems. She needed to act wisely rather than as a fool if it was her goal to restore her relationship with Simone, Eugenia, and the teen boys she was accused of offending. She wrote notes of apology and placed them in her laptop case to mail the next day. She still had more questions than answers, such as what Della had to do with all of this. Perhaps sheer jealousy. But she stopped that line of thinking and tried to maintain a spirit of reconciliation in her heart.

Cori then focused on her observations from the day's work. She typed up an outline of her Wednesday goals on a template she found particularly useful, took some melatonin for sleep insurance, and went to bed.

CHAPTER 5

EVADE AND ESCAPE

The next day started with Byron and a continental breakfast of cranberry orange muffins and coffee in a nook of the hotel lobby.

"I think we can proceed through the day responding in much the same way as yesterday, don't you?" Byron asked Cori between bites.

"Yeah. To an extent. I don't think we would be doing our jobs unless we let the environment determine our focus. As I said, to an extent. But I think if we're going to reach Anderson's friends—or cohorts, as they might more accurately be described—I'm going to be a bit more proactive."

"How are you going to do that?"

"I sent them passes to come see me."

"What makes you think they'll show up?" Byron asked.

"I don't, I guess. I can hope. Regardless, it's all information."

"Why are you forcing the issue? What if they just aren't ready or never need to talk about it?"

"Are you a reporter now or something? How? What? Why?" Cori laughed. "Sorry. You're right. If they really don't need it, so be it. I guess I just want to make sure. I'll admit it. I'm really after information."

"Who's the reporter, huh?" Byron laughed. "Just be careful."

"Why are you worried about safety if there is nothing to this?"

Byron simply finished chewing, offering no response.

When they arrived at school, Cori stationed her laptop, notebooks, and notes in the small conference room in which she had worked the day before. She then went to talk to Langston, the executive director, just to check in.

"Good morning," she said.

"Oh, good morning, Cori." Langston looked up from the counter in the main office, where he had been reading some lists, it appeared. "I hope you are comfortable in your lodgings."

"Yes, yes. They're very nice. Thank you. I was wondering if you know any more about whether Anderson's closest friends have been seeking support."

"I am checking that now. I'll let you know if I find there is a need."

She had an affinity for the director; she could tell he was somewhat of a softy. She wondered if he had received any pushback on the matter from friends or faculty. Well, if he didn't help, Cori thought, she could find ways.

Cori returned to the conference room to find a student waiting for her. The girl was extremely shy, and her eyes were red and moist.

"Good morning. I hope I haven't kept you waiting. I'm Cori. It's good to see you."

The girl quietly said, "Hello. I'm Etta." She said nothing else.

Etta reminded Cori of Della. She was just a slightly older version. Etta wasn't wearing the latest in designer clothes, which was another reason Cori felt an immediate camaraderie with her.

"I'm sorry, but I'm not really here about sadness over this guy, Anderson," Etta began. "I think it's awful what happened to him, don't get me wrong. But I just wanted to talk to someone who isn't a part of the school."

Cori responded immediately. "That's fine, Etta."

"OK. Good. Thank you." She paused, seemed to take a breath. "I hate school. Every minute that I'm here, I can't wait to get home. I'm not like anyone here. I have one or two friends, but we only see each other at lunchtime. I don't think the teachers even see me. I just feel like a nothing. I'm not a good student. Schoolwork seems meaningless. I try, but I just don't feel like doing the work."

There was a pause, so Cori responded. "Etta, I don't blame you for not wanting to be here, given the way you feel. What one change would help, if we could do one thing?"

"I want to be homeschooled."

Cori countered, but just a bit. "OK. Imagine you are homeschooled. Tell me about all of the ways that feels better."

Etta stared at her, then cracked a smile. "Well, I might feel more like I belonged. But I wouldn't have any more time with my friends. I probably wouldn't like the work any better. But I wouldn't feel criticized all the time, or invisible if I'm not being criticized."

Cori continued for her. "So, not perfect, but better?"

"Maybe."

Cori asked another question. "If you thought it through and it really seemed as though studying at home would be much better, is it possible?"

"Probably not."

Cori made a suggestion. "How about we talk about what might make this place better for you?"

"Yeah. Sure." It was drawn out; Etta seemed skeptical.

"Are you on social media with your friends?"

"What good would that do?"

"It might not. But what if you were in contact more often than just at lunch? When you are able to meet face to face, you could pick up where the e-contact left off."

"I don't have money for Internet access."

"Are you near a library? Do you have free time in school?"

"Yes. Both."

"Do you think you're willing to try?" Cori paused. She had another avenue to explore. "Etta, do you ever stay after school for help?"

"That doesn't sound like fun."

Cori laughed. "I know how it sounds, really I do! But teachers have a lot of students. You buy a lot of cred by showing *teachers* attention. The connections with them, and with your work, might just change. I predict you'll feel better about both. I think your teachers will notice as well."

"There's no reason not to try." Etta sighed deeply, but did seem somewhat committed. "I can use the school's computers after school, too."

"Good point!"

Cori had one more suggestion. "Etta, I just met you, so this may not seem appropriate, but you've been feeling this way for a long time. Is that right?

"Uh-huh."

"It's possible, over time, for those feelings to have led to a slight depression."

"Oh yeah. There's no doubt I'm depressed."

"Please give your school counselors some consideration. I've met both of them, and they really care about students."

"I don't think they have time for me."

"I can guarantee they do." Cori smiled.

When the bell interrupted their time together, Etta jumped up.

"Thank you. I need to get to my next class. I'm having a test."

"Sure. Thank you for the chat, Etta. I enjoyed meeting you. Please rely on your teachers. They're here to teach you. Go to them! And your school counselor can give you information on help for the depressed feelings you're experiencing. It really can make a difference. Promise?"

"Sure. Really, I will."

Cori felt sad that the school environment was toxic for some students and had become, seemingly, the worst thing in their lives. She was concerned for Etta, but also intended to check out her apprehensions about the deceased's friends. She was on her way to see if Langston had any more information when she met him coming toward her conference room. They slipped inside. He furrowed his brow as if concerned. Cori couldn't tell whether it was put-on.

"All of the students one would expect to make use of the grief counseling signed out of classes yesterday—many of them numerous times," he began. "So far, I haven't found that any of them have accessed an identified counselor. Technically, this is a truancy issue, so I have every right to follow up to see where they have been. I'm not interested in sanctions per se, but I am concerned."

Cori sensed that he wouldn't consider sanctions under any circumstances, but that was none of her business, nor did she care about other circumstances. She did care about who these students were spending time with, and she had her suspicions. "Thanks. Please let me know what you find out."

At that moment, a student appeared at the room entrance with one of Cori's passes. Seeing her through the small glass opening, Cori opened the door. "Come on in," she said.

"Hello, Georgia," Langston said. "It's good to see you. I'll be getting back to my office now."

Georgia was striking in every way. Her illusion of a wash-and-wear appearance was betrayed by her stylish and expensive clothes and accessories. She exuded confidence and, at the same time, there was quite an edge to her.

"Thanks for coming, Georgia. I'm anxious to get to know you and find out how to best meet any needs you or your friends have right now."

Georgia was sharp. "You don't have any reason to be concerned about me or my friends. We're getting all the help we need from people we've known for a long time. There isn't any need for us to talk with people we don't even know."

Cori didn't miss the chin flick. Some adolescents had that one perfected! Georgia's edge was even sharper than first perceived.

"Do you know of anyone who does need a bit of support?" Cori expected that Georgia would take this "poison pill" rather than talk to her about Anderson. This also was a predictable adolescent response to an adult's probe for information.

"No need." Open hostility was all that was coming from Georgia.

Cori switched gears. "This is a beautiful area of the country. I understand why skiing would be a passion. What's your unique contribution to the ski team?"

"I'm one of the only jumpers. And there aren't that many schools that participate in jumping, but there are a few. Even if we have to travel, we have a lot of competitions. I've been jumping since I was a little kid. I know it's a long shot, but I'm planning to study abroad where I can get even more practice time than I do here." This obvious improvement in attitude was allowing Georgia to chat for at least a bit. "Anderson was good for the team. He was fast. The faster the better. He loved the thrill and risk. We already had started to prepare for the season with sessions on conditioning, diet, and team building, that sort of thing. Anderson was really good, and he knew it."

Once again, the bell ending the period brought them back to reality—and Georgia's edge returned.

"I have to get back to class. We're going to be fine. You can leave us alone."

Cori was confident that the ski team had circled the wagons emotionally. Georgia's visit seemed to confirm this suspicion. Cori was more curious than ever and told herself she needed to find out what they had to hide.

Who else to turn to but "the bosses"?

She rushed to the main office. "Hey there. May I bother you for a copy of the most recent yearbook?"

"Sure. We have one under the counter here." An assistant got up from her chair, fetched the annual, and handed it to Cori.

She thumbed through it until she found a picture of the ski team. Not surprisingly, most of the names were familiar to her already as identified friends of Anderson. Cori was familiar with the coach because he was also the athletic director. He was one of the individuals who left the faculty meeting on Monday without joining a support group. In fact, she remembered her impression that he seemed to be leading the way for others in that group. She surmised that he was the go-to in the building and possibly aiding and abetting this wagon circling. A stronger leader would know this and get to the heart of the matter. She doubted Langston had it in him.

Cori's curiosity had given way to full-blown suspicion. Suspicion of what, she had no clue. She knew that normal didn't apply in a tragedy like this. But in her experience, human behavior isn't all that complex—unless someone works hard to make it that way. Simply put, one would expect at least some of these students to access or respond to offers of help in some way.

She couldn't think of anything clearly until she could schedule a meeting with the AD/coach, who she found out from "the bosses" was also a phys ed teacher. She found out his room number, but by this time the bell had indicated a new class was about to start. She decided to wait until the next full passing time, when he likely would be in his office. Instead, she set out to find Byron.

She found her coworker surrounded by a group of adoring coeds. She peered through the door glass but decided not to interrupt. Byron was very attractive to these girls! He was an excellent counselor as well, and that probably was why so many girls were now gathered around him.

She also knew that scenery counted—both to her and to much younger versions of herself!

CHAPTER 6

THE UNDERBELLY

Cori decided she had nothing to lose by finding out more about what might be hidden parts of the school and its culture. One of her father's closest friends had risen through the ranks and retired as a public school superintendent. He had determined that the underbellies of the school were the faculty room, the lunch room, and the bars where locals hung out and chewed the fat about high school sports teams. Without question, the bar would have to wait, probably forever, and the first lunch wasn't for nearly another hour.

As Cori entered the faculty room, all chatter subsided.

"Good morning!" She greeted the folks warmly. "I was looking for a coffee machine." She grabbed a cup and awkwardly sat down in the thick of the crowd sitting in easy chairs. The group was surprisingly larger than she would have anticipated. The easy chairs formed a large rectangle around a long table and chairs, which also were full.

"We haven't been told much about you and Byron," one of them, sitting next to Cori, offered. "Do you do this kind of work often?"

"Before we came, we said to each other that we're thankful not to have dealt often with the suicide of a young person. Our firm consults on a range of issues. Most people are familiar with community crisis and employee assistance counseling. We also do interviewing related to research, community building, and organizational development. Most of us are counselors, but we also have a legal team and MBAs."

"How long have you been doing this?" another asked.

"About six years."

She was relieved when the focus was thrown away from her, and typical gossip resumed.

"You know the Millers have another one in high school now," she heard from one small group. "He's just as lazy as the others. Almost a term has gone by. No homework, no classwork, and I've tried three times to contact the parents. Nothing."

Another conversation, concurrent to the other, was taking place. "Jeremy's on the suspension list. The kids said he was caught with pot after school in the gym. Again."

"I had to send Cully to the office again today. I tried every trick in the book to get her settled, but it just wasn't working. I came this close to sending her to the nurse. Another night of drinking, I suppose."

"What do you think they'll do about it?"

"Oh, nothing. But at least I was able to teach my class."

Cori cringed. She had encouraged Etta to spend time with these folks! She picked up the local paper to make it appear as though she wasn't listening. Her ploy worked.

"What's up with the kids on the ski team? They're acting as though they're part of the woodwork, not grieving the loss of their friend and a member of the team."

"Yeah. They're usually prancing around here like they own the place, which I guess they do. Now you'd hardly know they're here."

"Any time I see one of them, they're headed to Barrett's office."

Cori momentarily stopped breathing. *Barrett.* Why hadn't she noticed that was the same last name as the local police chief?

The faculty quips continued. "Don't you think it's quite a coincidence that Barrett's brother stepped in and took over the investigation? Investigation. That's a laugh."

"Do you think they're hiding something?"

"I wouldn't have thought anything about it if Barrett's brother hadn't stepped in. There may be nothing to it, but it just looks bad. I never could figure out why people do stuff like that."

"The dean of students told me that Barrett requested a guest teacher all week. Makes him quite available for chitchats with the kids, doesn't it?"

Cori nearly gasped when she noticed how much time had passed, so she finished her coffee and returned to her designated spot. She felt a little guilty about how little counseling she had done, and she began to doubt why she was acting like some sort of amateur sleuth. What did sleuthing have to do with why she was here?

A few girls and a guy were waiting outside her door.

"Come on in. It's good to see you today. I'm Cori. Thanks for coming by. Am I speaking with all of you at once?"

They looked around at each other even as they were taking their seats, and eventually they started to nod, all while looking a little confused. *Herd mentality—another adolescent trademark*, Cori thought.

"I ask because it doesn't impact confidentiality from my

point of view, but it's impossible for me to control what someone else is willing to keep in confidence."

Most of them mumbled their assent.

After they exchanged a number of glances with each other—almost as if they were silently passing the buck—someone finally spoke up. "We didn't really know Anderson all that well. It would be impossible to be in this school and not know who he was, though. It really is sad that he's dead. His family must be so shocked. He probably had friends who are really sad too. I don't know what I would do if that happened to someone I know."

"Yeah." One of the others joined in. "We can't figure out why someone would do such a thing. You just never expect it to happen around here."

"We knew the group he hung around with because some people thought the ski team was pretty important to the school," another said. "We didn't care all that much—is that OK to say? But we thought they all were happy. How could we be so wrong?"

Cori had no intention of being an answer person. "Anderson's death took everyone by surprise, it seems. And yes, it is unusual for a suicide to occur under those circumstances. Your feelings are perfectly valid. If this can come out of the blue, what else is lurking in the days and years ahead? Is that how you're feeling?"

"Yeah."

"Exactly."

"What are we supposed to do?"

Cori knew the answer had to come from them. "What would give you the most peace right now?"

"For something like this never to happen again."

"You want back the feelings you had before this occurred," Cori softly said. "What were they?"

"Safety. Happiness. Confidence."

"For whatever it is worth, I give you permission to feel that way again. Feel free to talk about this, or not. Take all the time you need to process—or none at all. And please be realistic about your safety. Accidents happen, but quite infrequently. It's rare, but sometimes people harm themselves. You're probably very accurate in thinking that it doesn't happen around here. Now that it has, it doesn't indicate that this will be a common occurrence. Whenever you're ready to be safe, happy, and confident again, go right ahead! I think you'll be choosing well."

Cori sensed her reassurances working, at least for the time being, and the group seemed more willing to talk about Anderson and less about the fact that their safe world had been shattered.

"He really was a good athlete. People thought he was really smart, too."

"Yeah. But I think he was better at finessing good grades than earning them," another said.

The latter comment came from a girl who had been silent until this point. It was apparent she was quite intellectual and knew what it was like to earn good grades.

"His friends must be really sad. They're not acting like they used to. The ones I've seen are signing out of class immediately, even before classes start. Usually they kind of horse around in the hallways. You know. High fives and all that. But they're not that way anymore."

Eventually, some of the girls in the group said they had to prepare a table during lunch for newspaper submissions; all of them politely left.

"Thanks for talking with us," Cori said as they made their way out.

The one male in the group stayed, and Cori felt a little taken back. His name was John. He appeared agitated and cleared his throat before speaking. His index fingers formed an inverted V in front of him on the table, and he tapped them rapidly.

"Should I say something if I think this is all crap?" John blurted out. He had Cori's attention! She knew there was a lot to unpack from that one sentence, and she wanted to give him full freedom to express his views.

"Of course," she said. John looked for a moment as though he would bolt. He was shifting in his seat, sighing. He rubbed his head and murmured, "Oh man." He didn't direct the comment to Cori. Just when Cori thought he would take off—this was when he really got started.

"Anderson was a selfish, bullying SOB who made my life miserable," John said. "I can't even imagine someone so full of himself taking his own life. What the hell were the signs, anyway? None that any of us could see!" John raised his voice a bit, and he didn't wait for an answer.

"What about his friends? What's their story?"

Cori was as doubled-minded at this moment as ever she had been. She was anxious to gain more information from John, but he obviously needed his feelings toward Anderson acknowledged. Honesty in details is of great importance to young people in times of tragedy, and this young man seemed unconvinced of the information being fed to him and his fellow students. Cori happened to agree with how he was feeling about this, but couldn't say that to him.

"Your feelings are valid and need to be heard," she said. "Please don't shut down before you've been able to say whatever is on your mind."

"No. I'm done. But thank you for listening. I wouldn't dare say any of those things to anyone other than a stranger—even the girls that were here before."

"It must be really uncomfortable with all of the attention being focused on Anderson. It may seem as though he is being lionized these last few days."

"You must think I'm awful for talking about him this way. But I'm just not buying any of it."

"Do you have an alternate theory for what happened?"

"No freaking idea."

"I know that's not up to you, and that wasn't a fair question. I want to keep your comments in mind as I continue to counsel. I wish I could share your views."

"You can share my views all you want. But, please, do not use my name! I don't think anyone will figure out who said it if you don't. I'm not the only one who hated the kid. He was such a jerk to so many people."

"Thanks, John. You've helped me a lot. I wish I could have done the same for you."

"Don't worry. I feel better. Uh . . . bye."

Adolescent awkwardness, Cori thought. She loved it. It should be accepted by adults more freely. She hated the ridicule teens or even adults would heap on one another.

Cori softly tapped her fingertips on the table for a few seconds, as if it would help her solve an inscrutable problem. Anderson obviously engaged in more than trolling these students. She suspected it went beyond micro-aggression as well. The irony of identifying bullies in an atmosphere of no-name-calling wasn't lost on her. Since it was fashionable, that's exactly how she identified Anderson—to herself. But maybe it was better to just simply say he engaged in bullying.

If only John had drawn a conclusion for her, even it was way off. *Did he suspect murder? An overdose?* Neither seemed even a remote possibility given the reading of the police report. She suspected something other than suicide. After a deep breath, Cori once again thought about how much they needed the coroner's report. She had no clue how she would obtain it, but that was a matter for another day.

Having amassed all the suspicion she needed, she abandoned the idea of hanging out in the cafeteria. She searched for Byron, who wasn't in his designated area. Her next stop was the proverbial corner office with "the bosses."

"I was wondering if I could look through the school pictures. Were there any taken this year?" Cori asked the women, a lilt in her voice. She was so comfortable with these women.

"Absolutely. Would you like to take them back to your space?" one of them answered.

"Yes. Definitely. Is that OK?"

"It's no problem. We have several copies, and they're uploaded to the database as well."

"OK. Great! But I'll get them back to you as soon as possible. You're the best."

Did Cori see another wink? They obviously got a kick out of her and took her seriously at the same time. It appeared to be a mutual admiration thing between them.

She started to pore over the pictures after she returned to her designated space. Some students came by to chat, so she set the pictures aside. The students were unsettled by the impact of the news at school, yet they were content to say their pieces and leave. She didn't know how long Byron had been waiting by the door, but he entered quietly right after the students left.

"So, were you able to tear yourself from your many admirers?" Cori was determined to have a good time teasing Byron about his popularity with the teen girls.

"I don't think that's what's going on. I'm sure you were giving solace in the same way I was."

She chuckled. "Byron, I know what I saw." Even as she teased him about the situation, her attention was drawn to her search through school portraits of Anderson's friends.

"What are you doing?"

"Well, the yearbook picture of the ski team was from last year's season. They were in their ski team garb, and I just wanted to see something more recent."

"What do you think you'll get from pictures, Cori?" He paused; Byron obviously thought Cori was taking an unnecessary step. "Oh, and I wanted to talk to you about identifying some social service agencies in the area tomorrow. Maybe meet with some and hand over the torch, so to speak. Since the funeral isn't until Saturday, I think we can prepare them for that and let them take it from here."

She heard him, but didn't respond. Grabbing picture after picture, finally she said, "Byron. Look at these pictures. Look at what almost all of them are wearing!"

He moved closer to her and gazed where she was pointing. "What? Are you talking about the turtlenecks? Some are wearing ties, too."

"Yeah. Are turtlenecks even a thing? And look at the other students. How many turtlenecks do you see?"

"Well, I'm not seeing any so far." He leafed through the pile. "I do see a few ties. What's the matter with . . . ? Oh no, Cori. What are you thinking? They were intentionally covering their necks? I thought you might be suspicious of an overdose and cover-up, but this? Are you out of your mind?"

"Hang on. I have to make a call."

Cori went to the phone and, after dialing, said, "Hi, Margie. It's Cori. Thanks for letting me borrow the school pictures. When did you say they were taken?" There was a pause. Cori seemed to repeat what Margie was saying. "So, two weeks after school started. That's about September fourteenth or so? Do you remember what kind of weather you had during the first couple of weeks of school?" Again, a pause. "Fairly warm until the beginning of October, huh? OK. Thanks! Again, you've been a big help."

Byron was truly agitated. "Cori, there's no evidence to support this. All you know is that most of the ski team wore turtlenecks or neckties in warm weather for the school pictures. It doesn't necessarily mean they were covering bruises from an extremely risky form of self-gratification. That's far-fetched. Let it go, please."

This wasn't the first time he begged something like this from her.

Seldom did Cori listen.

Her condo was somewhat in disarray in spite of her time spent "tidying up" just before they left. She gave in to the fact that she would be living in a mess for a while due to the fallout from weeks spent planning The Gathering. Computers were great, but she inevitably printed out lists, telephone numbers, templates for documents, and "to do" lists that just kept coming to mind. She still had the thank you notes to take care of—maybe tomorrow would be a good day for those. Would it take her mind off Byron's coldness, Simone's anger, the teen's overdose, and her obsession with the Stowe area case?

That's the answer. She needed distractions. The stranger had been on her mind. More than she would like to admit, she succumbed to daydreams about him. *Did he live in town? Was he just passing through? What was the basis for his expertise with the overdose?* Would she ever know?

Cori pulled together a plan for the next day, then decided to watch some television. Besides her silly thoughts about the stranger, she was finding little refuge from her inner confusion. But more and more Christmas images were appearing on television, and the DVR had collected Christmas movies and crime dramas over the last several days. Maybe that would help her unwind and peel off some layers of stress!

* * * * *

Cori began the next day using templates for thank you notes and creating new notes where necessary by cutting and pasting texts from other original documents. She also started on her draft of the report that would have to be polished off Monday with Byron. She felt as though she was creating fiction. It was the worst report she ever had drafted. She hoped that Byron had more productive sessions to summarize—or at least *something* better to report.

Now that she was home, Cori also had to find out what was

going on with the overdose victim and Simone. Maybe a few days apart had helped quell the storm with Simone. She probably would be at the church planning for that night's youth meeting, so why not call?

"Hey, Cindy. This is Cori. I was wondering if Simone is there?" The church secretary asked Cori to hold for a moment before returning to the phone.

"Ah, Cori. Simone can't talk right now. She wanted me to ask you to bring by any materials you have for your youth group that the church owns and leave them at the church office by Monday. Simone has found someone else to cover your meeting Monday night."

"Cindy. What's going on?"

"Really, Cori. I don't know. I thought you would know, so I didn't ask any details." There was a long pause between them.

Cori finally said, "Cindy, I don't know what to say!"

"Neither do I, Cori. I really don't know what's going on. Please, can I leave this between you and Simone?"

"Yes. But I think she and I need to talk. Please ask her to call."

"I will, Cori. Take care."

If Cori hadn't been sitting down, she would have collapsed. Instead, her body went limp. Could Simone really have removed her from the youth group?

CHAPTER 8

PARANOID MUCH?

Cori was not just stunned, she was rabid. The only good thoughts she could summon were for her brother and his wife and the kids in her youth group—or what used to be her youth group. Everyone else was more of a mess than she was, in her opinion.

Her anger solidified her opposition to Byron and his namby-pamby response to the Stowe area case. *The Stowe case.* That's where she would throw her energy for the time being, she told herself. *Who cares what Byron thinks? Who cares what anyone thinks!*

As hotheaded as she was, she knew she didn't want to jeopardize her job. Though Friday should have been R&R following her travel time, and it was getting rather late in the day, she went into the office.

"Hi, Sally. How are you doing? Is anyone in the legal

department?" The receptionist answered quickly, having noted that Cori was not her usual chatty self. She checked the schedule. "Go ahead, to the third floor. Someone should be available to see you."

Claris was a lawyer and oversaw many different aspects of the services provided at Amity. "Come on in, Cori," she greeted her. "How are things? Long time no see!"

"I know. Things get out of control very quickly, don't they?"

"They do for sure. I haven't had the opportunity to tell you what a great event The Gathering was. Also, how is that brother of yours and his bride?"

"Roman and Ainsleigh are doing so well. I can't tell you how happy I am to see the two of them together. I wish they weren't so far away!"

"How about their health, Cori? I know they're inherently good for each other, but has marriage caused a strain on the health of either?"

"I had the same worry. They are so good at supporting each other. The therapies take a lot of time, but they are devoted to doing their best. Ainsleigh tires easily. But I think she has a good sense about the amount of rest she needs in order to pursue her priorities."

"You don't think she's pregnant, do you?"

"Ah, no. One of the many details we were told all along was that males with CF often are unable to have children. Roman has known that for a long time. Ainsleigh actively sought dating matches online for someone with chronic disease. There are times she is nearly debilitated with chronic fatigue, so she also entered the relationship not only knowing she shouldn't jeopardize her health, but also knowing full well there was very little hope of conceiving. They are an amazing couple.

"Anyway, Claris, how are you? What's new in your life?"

Claris chose to follow Cori's lead and changed the subject from Roman and Ainsleigh. "I went on an exhausting, fantastic trip to Belize. The purpose was to provide pro bono work for an American mission there. But the work was very straightforward, and I wore myself out taking kids from their orphanage to the beach, of all things! What a blast. Since returning to work, it's been just that. Work!"

"I didn't know about the trip. Well done!" Cori paused and continued with her purpose in visiting Claris, not that she didn't love getting caught up. "Claris, I want to ask about legal obligations as well as legal restrictions that pertain to my last assignment."

"OK. That was with Byron, correct? Does he want to join us?"

"Ah . . . no. He wouldn't support me in what I want to do."

"And that would be . . . "

"First, I need to run a scenario by you that may require a mandatory report to child services in the Stowe area."

Cautiously, Claris said, "Go ahead."

Cori told her about the significant folks in Anderson's life, as well as those on the periphery, all claiming there had been no mention of self-harm in Anderson's history. "He was talking about college, practicing with the ski team, and there had been no change in his classroom misbehaviors or his supercilious attitudes toward students not in his circle of friends."

"I assume there's more."

"There's a lot more," Cori continued. "Don't pass judgment yet, please. As I said, he was on the ski team. School pictures taken in mid-September show the vast majority of the ski team in turtlenecks and a few in suits and ties. No one from the general pop wore turtlenecks; a few wore ties."

"So, their throats were covered. I sense what you're suspecting." At least Claris was willing to admit it! "Do you have more than that?"

"The friends wouldn't talk to us. They were almost

constantly out of class talking with their coach, who also is the athletic director. The athletic director was one of the first ones called to the scene by folks who reported the death, and he's also the brother of the chief of police, who took over the investigation and wrote the police report, even though he wasn't initially on duty when Anderson was discovered."

"Well, that hand off shows a conflict of interest as well as their stupidity and lack of ethics," Claris said. "But I'm getting ahead of myself. Cori, tell me what you would say if I were a social worker and you were reporting the incident? Sadly, Anderson is gone. What do you see as the danger to underage kids?"

Neither of them were going to put a name to what they perceived was going on.

"I think possibly it could be a ring or group involved in the risky behavior," Cori said. "I perceive the AD knows about it, at the least; he may have more involvement than that. If my suspicions are real, we know the behavior could become addictive. Somewhere I heard it said that the last stage of addiction is death. And one has already occurred."

Claris drew a deep breath, closed her eyes, and then spoke as if narrating her thoughts. "What we perceive and what we know are two different things. If we sense it, might not others also sense it and at least be willing to look into it?"

Without receiving an answer, Claris continued. "Let me think this through. I don't think anyone would see your perceptions as proof enough for you to have to report it to child services. But you could make a voluntary report. It could lead to something more concrete, which I think we need. Unless the coroner also is a good ol' boy, maybe that report could be helpful."

"Exactly. That was going to be my next question. Do we have any standing to request the coroner's report?"

"I can try." There was a long pause. Finally, Claris added,

"Cori, you look tired—at best. Please go home and try to rest. If you do anything work-related, let it be no more than the voluntary report, if you decide to submit it. If I conclude there is anything we can do, let's go up there as soon as possible."

Cori was so grateful for Claris. Maybe there was one other person on earth who wasn't, it seemed, making her a target.

"Thanks, Claris. I appreciate not only the walk-in appointment, but some confirmation of my suspicions."

"Cori, thank you for caring and not cowering."

Cori returned to her apartment. *Roman. How long since they had a really good talk?* They chatted right after The Gathering because she knew he would listen. She so wanted to see him. Quickly, she texted her brother that she might be traveling again with work and would like to talk before she left.

Before long, they were video chatting. "Hey, sis. I was surprised when you said you might be returning to the same site where you just served. That's unusual, isn't it?"

"Yeah. It is. I'll tell you about it sometime when you have a leisurely two hours. But there's a bit of unfinished business that would be best completed right away. How are you guys?"

"Actually, I wanted to check out something with you," Roman said. "Ainsleigh wants to visit you and see more of the New England area. We were thinking about Thanksgiving. I thought Ainsleigh would love Briny Bluffs Resort for the same reasons we do. Probably Simone's family would be OK with two more. They're always a hoot! You will be going again this year, right? So, is it OK if we ask to join you?"

"So . . . " Cori invoked her usual stalling tactic for when she needed time to think. She had thought about what she would say to Roman about Simone, church, and everything, but she still hadn't decided on her exact approach. "About that." Deciding not to address the full picture at this point, she simply said, "Simone's family isn't going this year. I was surprised. I hadn't landed on any concrete plans, but I had mused over the fact that I still could go. I have some time coming, so why don't we?"

"Wow. I can't believe Simone's family would drop it like that. But your plan sounds good. I'll make our reservations and plans to fly directly there."

"OK, Roman. But you'll drive back with me to stay a few days in Laurel Ledge, right? You can make your return flight to Arizona from Hartford. I can't wait to see you both! We'll talk again soon."

Cori held out her right fist and yanked it back toward herself. "Yes. I like this plan."

* * * * *

Cori's come-down came soon. She knew of no one who looked forward to making a report to child services. The agency is one of those entities for which one is thankful and yet feels leery about at the same time. The task of reporting was always something to loathe. It took Cori only a quick online search before she had the number and fax. She dialed and asked for intake.

Immediately, she heard "Intake," and Cori began her story all over again. The pause and lack of questions made it obvious the intake worker was astounded at her suspicions. For a good bit of the time, Cori sensed that the person on the other end was cautious of a punch line and hoped that this was a crank call. It all definitely felt awkward. At a point, though no specific terms were used, the intake worker knew exactly what Cori was alleging. She asked very few questions, other than demographics, and asked for a written report within forty-eight hours.

Cori resolved to get the report done right away. She found the template from the same website she had accessed earlier, wrote her findings, and faxed it to the number provided.

Then she emailed Claris to let her know, and asked if she wanted a copy.

In all that had been said, no one had used a hot-button term.

But she had to put it in writing.

CHAPTER 9

No Happy Hour Here!

Claris had been a New York county assistant district attorney before moving to the private sector. When she accepted the position in the legal department at Amity, she understood she would wear many hats. One of the possible roles was investigative work, for which there would be an occasional need. Until now, however, that need had not come to fruition.

Claris was like Cori in many ways, and one of their many similarities was being able to sense when someone shared a kinship. Both Claris and Cori kicked into gear when they perceived an injustice—especially one that was overlooked or intentionally ignored by the majority of folks. While respectful, neither cozied up to power for their own gain, and both were willing to call into account any apparent abuse of power.

Perhaps both were viewed by others as going a bit overboard.

They each had an inkling that it made them unpopular, and they both cared. But neither resolved to change.

Claris felt a little guilty that she was energized by the prospect of becoming involved in an investigation. She didn't think, however, this colored her ability to be rational. Truly, she sensed that something was awry as soon as Cori had informed her of the few facts they had to date.

At best, their suspicions were unfounded. At worst, they could be treading into a situation they could make volatile for everyone involved, including Amity. Her first act upon Cori's departure was to email Amity's CEO about their suspicions and plans to follow up.

Her second act was to call a friend at the district attorney's office in the county where Amity was headquartered. Before doing anything else, she wanted to understand how another legal mind would see the circumstances.

Making a call like this on a Friday afternoon could make her one of the most hated lawyers in the northeast. No matter how busy the work week, Fridays after criminal court had concluded were sacrosanct. The legal community might get together and talk shop, but the talk was more analogous to gossip than work, and nearly always it involved what used to be referred to as happy hour at a local watering hole. Claris recalled many after work chat sessions in which parties around their group moved to other tables or asked if her companions could "keep it down." The DA's staff members often forgot how gross the topics of their conversations were to the outside world.

Finally, the ringing on the other end was answered, and her thoughts of the past were interrupted.

"Hi, Claris. Why don't you come over and join us?" His volume was louder than necessary, so she knew he was in a noisy lounge, as she had suspected. Trent was a former colleague, and though they were friends, they weren't able to connect as often as each would have preferred.

"Hey, Trent. Sorry to interrupt. I actually need to talk to you about something really confidential, so I don't think that would be a good setting. Are you able to talk for a minute privately?"

"Are you still in the office?"

"Yes."

"Why don't I come there?"

"That would be great. Are you sure you don't mind?"

"I hate to admit it, but this scene does get old after a while. I'd love to see you and find out what's on your mind."

"Wow. Thanks. See you soon."

"Be there in a half hour or so."

Claris tidied up a bit and closed out some of the work she had been sorting through when Cori came by. She also saw that Cori had emailed, so she quickly responded, answering that a fax of the report Cori prepared for protective services would be helpful. She told her to redact all names and locations before faxing—just for everyone's protection. She also opened an email from the CEO. It simply said, "Get a second opinion; tread lightly, and keep me informed."

Security called Claris upon Trent's arrival since it was now a bit after hours. "Go ahead, Henry. Send him up. I'm expecting him."

The bear hug showed how glad they were to see each other. They both started to speak at once and could hardly find a launching point for all the catching up they wanted to do. Claris was practical in her approach. "Why don't we talk shop first, and then go out to dinner to get caught up?"

"Sensational. So, what's on your mind?"

"Better that I show rather than tell." She handed him the fax. "Here is a redacted report one of the Amity counselors just sent to a small town in the Stowe area."

Trent sighed deeply and raised his eyebrows within a few seconds of reading the report. "I admit, you've thrown me a curve!" Then, a question: "Beyond the report, what do you think could be Amity's involvement?"

"My question exactly."

Trent breathed in deeply, pursed his lips, and said, "Then let's ask some questions."

They looked up the district attorney's office in the region. This particular DA presided over two counties, but there was a satellite office and courthouse very close to the school where Cori consulted. They made the call on Trent's cell, then set it on speaker.

"District Attorney's office." The person on the other end didn't sound happy.

Trent identified himself and his role and asked if an assistant district attorney was available.

"Speaking." The tone was no gentler than before.

"Sorry to be contacting you after hours on a Friday, but I'm looking for some advice on a situation that might be brewing in your district." Trent gave the few details they had.

The attorney heaved a sigh and said, "Yeah. Child services called me immediately, and I just got the report faxed to me. I recognized the area code; that's why I picked up the phone. I'm the only one left in the office, by the way. Anyway, the Department of Children and Families wants us to do a joint investigation with them. They're electing to screen in without any further evidence." They all were familiar with the process and knew that "screened in" meant there would be an investigation.

There was a long pause. Trent and Claris looked at each other, raised their eyebrows, and nodded as if both were relieved things were progressing—and seemingly so quickly.

Trent broke the silence. "That is obviously good news to us. Can we do anything to help?"

"I have more questions than answers at this point, obviously. But we'll definitely want an audience with this Cori as soon as possible. How about first thing Monday morning?"

"Assume that we can make that work. You'll be notified when she arrives in town. I have another question. Have you seen the coroner's report?"

"Personally, no. But I'm going to see it, and darn soon too." Only thing: he used a much more colorful adjective. He continued—with some additional colorful language—to emphasize how expedient the response needed to be.

"Hey man, thanks. I know how you must feel about this being dumped on you after hours on a Friday afternoon."

"You know it."

There didn't seem to be much of a basis for further discussion, so they made sure they had accurate names and contact numbers before ending the call.

Trent and Claris sat in silence for some time.

"We should call Cori," Claris said finally.

"Yeah. Of course." Trent thought for a moment and then said, "I'm going with you both."

Inwardly, Claris was relieved. The situation was creepy in spite of her penchant for solving crimes. But she wanted to be sure Trent really was OK with what he was doing.

"Are you sure? Should you run it by your office?"

"I'll tell them."

Claris chuckled. She knew he was a valued member of the office. Obviously, he could go off the reservation if he wanted to . . . occasionally.

Trent added, "Does Amity offer accompanying security when necessary?"

"Is it necessary?" Claris quickly asked.

"Don't know. If it's a big deal, we can skip it. I just have a hunch that it's a good idea."

"Yeah. We can do that. I'll get it going. Then, let's get some dinner."

They called Cori. Claris typed and printed a work requisition for a security detail beginning Sunday evening, then dropped it off with security on her way out.

She would tell Trent about her decision to leave on Sunday evening during dinner.

CHAPTER 10

PARANOID MUCH!

Cori was amazed at all the progress Claris had made in the short time since they had spoken. It was gratifying to be heard—and yet also horrifying, in a way, to realize how deep into this situation she had taken herself, especially by virtue of how many people were now involved.

Worried that she would doze off if she watched television, and too tired to start a project, Cori decided it was time to get some groceries for the next forty-eight hours. She knew this was one of the worst times for crowds at the market, but she would have to deal with it.

She was daydreaming while staring in the meat section when she heard her name. She turned to see Reina, Della's mom.

"Hey, Reina. This is so good. I've wanted to see you. How are you and Della?

"Della's good. Me too. She misses you at church, though."

Cori carefully avoided a discussion on her plans about church or what had happened. "I love my job, but that definitely is the down side. I have to be out of town so often. I really would love to have Della over to my place and spend time with her."

"She'd love that too! I've got to run, but can I give you my number so that if you find a convenient time, you can let me know?"

"Sure. And don't hesitate to call me too."

They quickly exchanged numbers, and Cori found out that Reina was just as comfortable with a text as a call. Good news! Her attention went back to the meat counter. Just a few seconds later, she heard her name again.

"Hey, Cori. How long has it been?" It was her thesis advisor from graduate school.

"Daphne! It seems like a lifetime since I've seen you. How are things?"

Daphne's demeanor changed quickly. "Cori, may I ask who you were talking with just now?"

"Her name is Reina, and I met her and her daughter, Della, through my former church youth group."

"I thought that's who it was. I'm very surprised to see her back in town."

"I didn't know they had lived in town before!" Cori didn't try to hide her surprise. "You seem concerned, Daphne. We've only been acquainted for a short time, but Della is very dear to me already. Is there something I should know?"

Daphne drew in a deep breath and looked pained. "I'm torn. I think you're just what they need, and I don't want to burden you with sordid history . . . unnecessarily."

"Now you have to tell me." Cori wasn't at all sure she really wanted to know, or would believe what could be tantamount to gossip. But separating herself from the importance of something just said to her—as in this moment—wasn't a usual action she took.

"Not here."

"Where?"

"The Sandwich Club?"

"Is that an appropriate place for this kind of a conversation? Any more so than here?"

"Once we get there we won't have to name names," Daphne said. "We'll know who we're talking about. Just for a little more background, it involves a doctor at Compass Points."

"You mean the pregnancy shelter?" When Daphne nodded yes, Cori couldn't help but think this wasn't good. She agreed to meet. Cori finished her shopping, sans perishables, and headed for the Club.

She ordered a shot of decaf with a sprinkle of cinnamon for a little pizzazz and then realized she hadn't eaten. Perhaps that had been the subliminal motivation for grocery shopping! So she ordered her favorite sandwich and found a seat.

Daphne arrived and joined Cori. She was acting quite antsy. "Go ahead and eat, Cori. I'm too keyed up to eat right now."

Cori took a sip of her coffee, and Daphne declared, "Maybe something in my hand will calm me down. I'll get a coffee. I'll be right back."

Cori focused on consuming as much as she could of her half sandwich to get it out of the way before Daphne returned. When they both were settled and sipping coffee, Cori said, "OK, Daphne. Please take your time, but spill it!"

Daphne began. "I think you'll remember when you were in grad school I was on retainer as a therapist at Compass Points as well as teaching in the counseling psychology department at the university. A very battered, pregnant woman came to the shelter one evening while I was there. We sensed she still was in danger, but her need for medical attention was a priority. The ER decided she should be admitted, but transported her for safety to another hospital to slow the attacker from finding her location. She lost the baby, but slowly recovered at Compass Points since she had no other place to go.

"I didn't continue as her therapist, but I did help her get a restraining order as soon she was released from the hospital. We were surprised that her batterer never seemed to try to find her. The police said they filed charges, but hadn't determined his location, so they couldn't arrest him or serve him with an abuse petition. My opinion is that he hightailed it out of town. If he had stayed around, he would have been facing some serious charges.

"She stayed at the shelter for weeks. She gained strength and eventually started job hunting and talking about apartment hunting. And then, suddenly, she became withdrawn and anxious. She no longer job hunted, and she locked herself in her room as much as possible. She refused to see the doctor though she was sick much of the time. I thought I had her convinced to see an outside doctor . . . when she disappeared.

"By the time she was gone, most of us suspected she was pregnant again. That's why I convinced her to see an outside doctor. There was no official word, but rumor had it that her condition was a result of someone at Compass Points. The suspected person not only continues to be there, but continues with behavior that is inappropriate with the women.

"I know this isn't incontrovertible evidence, but I find it easy to believe the rumors. You can bet that someone knows what happened. I also think his family is very powerful and made sure the woman we're talking about got out of town.

"You don't know how glad I was to see her and see how well she looks. But, I am shocked that she would return here."

Daphne stopped for a bit. "Cori. Say something."

"Daphne," Cori began, "I am so fed up with human beings that I want to scream. But, you're one of the good guys. Thanks for putting yourself out there and telling me about your suspicions. As I said, I'm just getting to know the young girl and her mom. Before you saw us, we were making plans to get together, and I intend to follow through. It might not be right away since I have a situation brewing at work."

Cori sympathized with the fact that Daphne was haunted by this situation. Now, so was Cori. She kept these thoughts to herself, but she was slowly forming a suspicion that folks might not be pleased with Reina's return. Perhaps her relationship with Reina and Della had something to do with Cori being shunned. She couldn't connect all of the dots, but she remembered that Simone had mentioned Della.

Cori felt so sad about all of it. The grief was too familiar, and it reminded her of the sorrow that had been so piercing at the prospect of losing Roman and those times when she had to face that his life would never be "normal." Over time, and with prayer, she had learned to redefine "normal"—as well as many of her priorities and expectations in life. All the same, processing grief and disappointment didn't come to her any more easily than it did anyone else.

Eventually, she came to accept God's will for Roman regarding his health. She understood that bad things happen. Perhaps it was hardest to accept the times when Roman was mocked and shunned for his differences. It was still difficult for her to deal with people intentionally inflicting pain—physical or emotional.

Cori told herself she needed to have faith and hope in this situation as well. She wasn't sure how to support Daphne, or how and when to end this encounter. "Daphne, I promise I'll let you know if I find out anything more about the Carbones. But I can't help but ask your opinion on why these issues with Compass Points haven't been addressed."

"I'd have to guess, since I ended my relationship with Compass Points the day Della's mom disappeared. I've wondered if there is anything I can do to bring the people responsible to justice. I just don't think I have enough information. Probably the real answer is these people are very powerful . . . in every way. Money. Status. Control. Favors. And obeisance for the favors. You name it."

Without realizing what she was saying, Cori responded, "I'll find a way. I hope you'll be willing to help if need be."

"You can count on it. Thanks, Cori. Bye."

Cori stayed behind for a bit and pondered the information she had just heard. She knew nothing about the players in this situation—except for Reina and Della.

Cori returned to her condo and decided to try sleeping. Thankfully, it worked.

* * * * *

On Saturday, she heard from Claris about arrangements for them to leave for the Stowe area Sunday afternoon. Cori spent the balance of the weekend reading and watching television. She wasn't in a mood to deal with people.

CHAPTER 11

THE SEDUCTION

Cori had been gung ho to help on the Stowe case just a couple of days before, but now she was too distracted by this newest twist in her life's path. She snapped out of it a bit when she stepped into the car that picked her up at the designated time on Sunday afternoon and saw not one person but three others in the vehicle. She was introduced to the assistant district attorney, Claris's friend Trent, and also the man hired for security, Stewart.

Stewart was chosen by the group to initiate the more detailed introductions to one another. "I worked for five years on the Cape as a cop and then a detective. The money was good given all of the traffic detail and overtime in the summer, but I quit because of all the traffic detail in the summer! I do private investigations and private security, for the most part. Whenever I don't have a gig, I write. I've published a bunch of articles. I have more than enough material for a book. I'll get an agent any day now. At least, that's what I keep telling myself. Never been married. No kids—I guess that's a good follow-up comment! I came to this area because of a big assignment with a client here a few years back. When that ended, I just stayed.

"Now, whose turn next?"

Trent volunteered. "Mine will be quick. I guess I'm a career assistant district attorney. I went to Western Massachusetts Law University for my law degree, interned with the county district attorney's office, they helped me get this job, and I've been here ever since."

"You all know my story, right? You can skip me." Claris tried this tactic, but it didn't work. "I moved to New York City after graduating from a small law school in California. After I passed the bar, I took a job with the Manhattan District Attorney's office. It was a great ride, but the commute was a killer. No pun intended, by the way. Even with that, I barely lived above the poverty level. The work was great experience, but I couldn't afford any of the amenities for which someone chooses the city. I didn't want to be a defense attorney since there are too many criminals I would refuse to represent! Working for Amity seemed perfect at the time. I really do like it. I just miss the intrigue, I guess. A little."

"I think you're all way too modest!" Cori said. "If you make me do this, no way I'm going to shorten the story of my life that much or focus only on my career."

All chuckled.

Cori continued. "I know it's awful to say, and I'm sure I wouldn't be able to make you understand, and I'm just being melodramatic, but my life really started when my brother, Roman, was adopted. If you know me, you know he is the passion in my life. I can't really remember much of anything before he came to us. He has a chronic lung disease, and his care enveloped my family life, or it seemed that way to me.

He required a gazillion hospitalizations and daily procedures to keep him breathing. I know I'm not telling this well, but I rarely resented anything involving his care. He has been such a joy in my life, truly.

"Our parents died while I was in college. I didn't realize how much of his care they provided until the sole responsibility was his and mine alone. But I managed to finish college and graduate school. Roman is married now. It's a miracle to see him so happy after all of the crap he's endured.

"I'm working on redefining myself! I'll let you know when I have a working theory!"

There was a very long silence.

"I'm sorry," Cori finally said. "The story of my life is always such a downer. I'm really OK about it. I apologize for introducing such a damper to the conversation. But, you did ask for it!"

They laughed. "Really, Cori. I know the Cori story, but I'm always taken back at the sacrifices you've made," Claris said. "So why have you chosen to run yourself ragged with The Gathering, the church youth group, your relentless pursuit of justice? I've always wondered why you didn't indulge yourself once you had the opportunity."

Cori's only reply: "I guess I want to do what I can. I don't think it's much."

They each had a room at a hotel that was selected for both its distance and proximity to the town in question. Not knowing what they faced, they thought a little distance from the actual town was wise, but they wanted to be close enough for ease of access as well.

The local assistant district attorney, Cliff Emory, joined them for an early dinner at a restaurant a few miles from their hotel. He seemed pleasant, and even in her present state of mind, Cori admitted to herself that it was fun sharing stories and enjoying some comic relief, jaded though it was. With two assistant district attorneys, one former ADA, and a private investigator, there were more than enough stories to go around. When Cori wasn't binge-watching Christmas movies in season, she was watching as many crime dramas as she could fit into her schedule. It was interesting to hear stories from folks who had lived some of the real thing.

Eventually, the conversation landed on what they all had in common. Stewart excused himself to provide the others with some privacy and went to the bar. Emory got down to business. "I finally saw the coroner's report. It took a long time for me to receive it, but not that long after I knew to request it!" He again used colorful language to further clarify his stance on the delay.

Emory continued. "The report clearly called for further investigation, and that is what I intend to do. For the time being, I don't want to taint what Cori might have to say during her interview tomorrow. An advocate will brief Cori on what is to be expected during a joint investigation by the state police assigned to my office as well as the social workers from child protective services. I think they plan on making a videotape."

Cori slouched in her chair a bit. "As much as I want to see this pursued, I'm beginning to lose my sense of adventure," she said. "I hope I can help."

Claris couldn't help herself. "Finally, you are becoming appropriately cautious, Cori!"

Cori chuckled and daydreamed for a moment about the matter at hand juxtaposed with finding out more about Reina and what she had been through. She felt herself slipping into a vindictive mind-set, caring not one way or another whether these spoiled teenagers faced the consequences of their stupid indulgences. She vacillated between trying not to succumb to those thoughts and actively summoning them up.

Emory left, and Cori's party went to find Stewart at the bar. They found some serious karaoke was happening, and they sat down to enjoy it. Cori never had performed, but always wondered what it would be like. She had a decent singing voice. Stewart seemed to notice her pensive smile and took a guess at what was on her mind.

"You've done this before?" He ventured a guess just to get things going.

"No. No. No. No. You've got that wrong. It's not my style."

"*You've* got it all wrong, missy. That's the whole point. You pick your own style with karaoke. Soprano or alto?"

She found herself responding without thinking. "Sort of in between. Second soprano."

"Which means you could do melody, right? I'm a bass. Think of a song with melody and bass."

She kept the conversation going in spite of herself. "Let Me Be There," she answered.

"Olivia Newton-John. Perfect. I'll get us in the queue."

Stewart was on his way before Cori could stop him. When he returned, he said, "Must not be a very adventuresome crowd. We're up next!"

Cori gasped. She really couldn't follow through. She was about to say so when he grabbed her hand and pulled her along. "We're up."

She was onstage. She heard applause. He handed her a mic. She took it. The music started. He pointed to her cue. She surprised herself when she started singing. She was hardly aware of how she was doing, but after a few notes Cori mustered up enough awareness to try her best. In that setting it seemed to be good enough, and as her experience became less surreal and more reality-based, she started enjoying herself. She also sensed that they sounded OK. She loved the song and became determined to have some fun with the opportunity to sing it.

Stewart was a performer. He danced circles around her, and he had a booming bass voice. He became the show, and all she had to do was sing her part. When it was finished, they grabbed each other in a side hug and laughed. There was a huge round of applause, so they continued laughing while taking a bow. There still was applause as they put the mics on their stands and ran offstage, only to return for another bow since the applause continued. There were a few calls for an encore, but Cori headed for her seat. They were still laughing, and so were Trent and Claris.

As things settled a bit, Claris said, "That's a side of you I haven't seen before!"

"Me either!" Cori quipped. They all laughed a good deal more.

"Why don't we do another one?" Stewart insisted. Cori shook her head decidedly: no.

"I don't know another one I would want to do. Anyway, I think we landed on the only perfect song for our individual ranges."

"Oh, so if we found another song, you'd be willing to do an encore? You've been thinking about this, I can tell."

"No, I haven't."

"You have. Come on. What would it be?"

She admitted she always wanted to sing "When Will I Be Loved?"

"Olivia Newton-John followed by Linda Rondstadt. Interesting. Good enough taste. I'll set it up."

"No."

Stewart was already on his way. Again, they didn't have to wait very long, and it went even better this time. There wasn't quite the hilarity; they were seasoned performers at this point, after all. They had a great time. The crowd seemed to love them. When they had taken their seats, the manager came over and introduced himself.

"I can't wait for this to get around. It's going to be great for business."

"You seem to do a good business as it is," Cori said,

complimenting him. It was a good-sized crowd.

"For some reason, Sunday nights are usually busy. People trying to escape the prospect of Monday morning, I guess. Anyway, what brings you in?"

"We're just visiting the area." Cori provided as little information as she could.

"Good. It's a great area to visit. How long will you be here?"

"We're probably leaving in the morning."

"Oh. Well, feel free to come back anytime."

"Thanks. It's been fun."

It was getting late, so they took care of the bill. Stewart seized the back seat with Cori on the return trip to the hotel. He sat decidedly closer to her than Claris had, and he seemed to find ways to touch her hand. Eventually, he just started holding it without any pretense. It was a little too soon for Cori's taste, but she didn't want to make too much of it. Besides, it felt good. She decided to enjoy it.

It was well after dark when they arrived back at the hotel. Stewart did the secure thing by checking the surroundings before the others got out of the car. He checked the lobby and elevator ahead of them as well. He kept a wary eye as they got into the elevator. They all said goodnight when they reached their floor, and the others departed for their respective rooms. Stewart followed Cori, making conversation the whole way.

They arrived at her room, and Cori spoke first. "I had a great time. I can't remember when I had that much fun, and you definitely were the catalyst behind it all. Thanks for challenging me to sing."

"It was great, Cori." He lowered his voice to a whisper. "In fact, you're great. You may not be able to remember when you've had this much fun, but I can't remember the last time I was this attracted to anyone."

He kissed her gently. He made a quiet groan and kissed her harder. She slowly felt her body meld into his. The feeling was irresistible, and she wanted more. She got more as she felt him rub her back and then press her to him. All at once his tongue was probing her mouth, and she responded.

He whispered her name while taking the magnetic entry card she had handy and began opening her door. It was then that Cori's bumpers went up, both physical and intellectual. It was one of the most difficult things she had ever done. Stewart met all of the criteria for a passionate one-night stand, but a one-night stand was on Cori's never-to-do list. Awkward as it was, she wrenched her way out of his arms and turned away from him.

"Stewart, I can't do this. I'm sorry if I misled you."

No way did she want to give up on him completely. She wanted to cushion the statement with how much she would like to see him again, but she knew she needed time. Yet, she couldn't seem to say anything.

Cori wasn't sure someone would ever meet her list of criteria. To further complicate the issue, one of the traits on her list was that *he* should have a list—and it might be hard for her to measure up in such case! As much as she wanted romance, she knew the inherent complexities in finding it.

Without any need for further explanation, Stewart responded like a complete gentleman. His tender smile and quick acquiescence to her wishes was at once a relief and a disappointment. But not really. What was she thinking she would do if he became insistent or obnoxious? He was the security detail!

They said a quick goodnight. Cori opened the door, but then became frozen in the contemplation of what had just occurred. When she failed to enter, the door slammed shut just after Stewart disappeared around the corner. She came out of her stupor and was about to open the door again when she heard a muffled voice in the distance. Curious whether someone had heard their conversation, she slipped quietly over to the hallway corner and peered around it.

It was Stewart walking away from the corner on his cell. "No. She backed out just as we were about to go in to her room. It was working until then. Sorry. I can try again if you want?" There was a quick pause and he said, "OK. I think you're right. I don't think this was the right time. See you when I get back."

Cori felt the blood drain from her head, face, and neck. She didn't want to imagine what that conversation was about or with whom it took place. She suddenly felt extremely vulnerable and foolish, and she hurried to her room, closing her door behind her ever so quietly. She went through all the motions of getting ready for bed, then went to bed. But there was no sleeping.

Cori's thoughts would not stop racing. There were endless scenarios that circled through her mind, but she could make no sense of any of it. For what insane reason was he supposed to have seduced her? She never used strong language, though she admitted that in some instances it served a purpose. She couldn't help but let "WTF" run through her mind. Repeatedly.

CHAPTER 12

DEFLATED

Cori woke up to a text from Claris. "Stewart discovered our tires have been slashed."

Cori panicked and her mind seemed to go berserk. She called Claris and launched in. "Just shows that something is up."

Claris corrected her. "It shows that they know we're here and why."

"I know, I know," Cori said. "It isn't tantamount to an admission of any culpability. But how brazen could they be? And just who are they?"

Cori took some delight in the fact that Stewart should be embarrassed that he failed to protect them. Well, truthfully, he failed to protect the car. She was quite open to finding any way to put him in a bad light. She knew she shouldn't and couldn't get "back at him." But she was going to let him know what she heard and, if he knew anything about her, she would keep going until she found out what was going on. After all, what did he think this trip was all about if not her tenacity?

Cori, Trent, and Claris met in the continental breakfast room. Trent called Emory, who informed them that his tires had been slashed as well. Rather than call the state police assigned to his office, Trent called the next district.

Emory got a ride with his wife and arrived at the hotel at just about the same time as the state police. He had called child protective services, and they were able to redirect the staff assigned to the case to the hotel. Though it was makeshift, the state police and social workers were set up in a conference room to question Cori.

The top-ranking officer, a major in the major crimes unit of the state police, was on site to oversee the case. He was a seasoned professional and stepped in seamlessly with appropriate questions relating to both the alleged suicide and the tire slashing.

Cori was relieved when the morning ended. She returned to her room while the others discussed next steps. She felt as though she had had enough. A text arrived just as she finished gathering herself. It was Claris. "Can you come back downstairs? We're going to the DA's office."

"What?" Cori responded.

"We'll have an escort."

"I'll be down."

The car's tires had been replaced, and Cori assumed Stewart was going to drive to an undisclosed location and wait for them. The other three loaded into the back of the unmarked state police cruiser, and they took off. In fact, it felt just like a takeoff. They were going 80 miles an hour in the left lane of the interstate in a manner of minutes. Needless to say, they arrived in a very short time.

Cori wasn't sure what was going on, but for once she

decided not to ask. She and Claris were ushered through a tiny hallway and into a small office. She thought perhaps it was a makeshift waiting room, but at least it was private. She was not impressed by the surroundings.

The walls were clearly paper thin. While waiting, both of them could overhear a conversation taking place in an adjacent office. A man was filling in a woman about juvenile court on the previous Friday. It was obvious the man wasn't the usual participant at the juvenile division. Apparently, the woman had Friday off, and he had been her substitute.

They weren't lawyers, so Cori assumed they were the advocates who helped victims and witnesses during court procedures. She recalled that Emory had suggested a victim advocate would brief her before the joint interview, but given the change of location, an advocate never surfaced.

"But your honor, my client is living in the youth facility and has been a model citizen there for over a week. It makes no sense to remand him to a more secure facility." The male advocate obviously was pitching his voice, mocking the young defendant's attorney, especially the part about being a model citizen since there had been so little time for the youth to have proven himself.

The dialogue continued when the female advocate said, "Is this the name of that juvenile defendant?"

It seemed to Cori and Claris as though the male took a brief look at a document, then said, "Yeah. That's the one."

"Wasn't he your victim in the superior court trial week before last?"

"Holy cow. You're right. I didn't even make the connection. He looked like a hunk of you know what on Friday, but he was all dressed up when he testified in superior court."

They both laughed, maybe a little nervously, and the male kept repeating, "Holy cow . . . holy cow."

Cori glanced at Claris, who winced and nodded yes. They

didn't want to make their presence known, but Cori took the gesture to mean that all aspects of the scenario they were listening to came with the territory. Cori imagined that it might be difficult at times to define victim and perpetrator. Obviously, one person could occupy both roles depending on the circumstances!

After a short period, Trent and Emory emerged from the latter's office. They invited both women in.

Behind the closed door, the local ADA explained that the trip to the DA's office was all for show. In case there was a mole, they wanted to show they planned to proceed. Emory thanked them for their willingness to go along with the plan without question.

Now that Cori had provided her oral statement, Emory was comfortable disclosing the rest of what he knew to this point. "The coroner's report was quite conclusive. This was not a hanging. The investigation would continue. I can't promise routine updates, but if and when there is a final disposition, you will know about it. If any court cases ensue, Cori could be called as a witness."

A few days before, Cori would have been disappointed to be dismissed like this at this point. But given all that was happening at home, and the unknown forces that seemed to surround them in the Stowe area, she was relieved. Emory wanted to maintain a front, for appearances, and it was late in the day, so he asked the group to spend one more night. He arranged a safe house through the State Police Major Crimes Division.

They were escorted out a different door from the one they had entered, and the car in which they traveled next didn't resemble anything like a cruiser. They arrived at what was essentially a palatial condo. Dinner was brought to them, and after eating they relaxed in the living room hot tub. Stewart, though, was nowhere around. It seemed he had left the picture.

The hot tub provided a good place for conversation, so

Cori asked Claris how she happened to connect with Stewart. Claris seldom needed to ask security for escorts, but she had started this process with them. After the tires were found slashed, and Stewart begged off the detail, Claris called the security office at Amity to attempt to vet the process of hiring Stewart for this job—albeit after the fact. She found out he had been pals with Henry, the head of security, so he seemed like an obvious choice for the trip. Claris wanted to know why Cori was asking. Cori told her what had happened in the hotel and explained that she thought it was an attempt to discredit her further with her church.

"You don't think it had to do with this case we're on?"

"I doubt it," Cori answered. "But I don't know for sure. The tone of the conversation I overheard seemed much more as if they were after a morals breach than to derail me from this case or bring me physical harm."

Claris was confused and told Cori so. Cori raised her voice a bit, saying, "So am I!" She told Claris a bit more about what was going on, then had one more important thing to say to her friend.

"One thing. You know I won't stop until I've found out, right, Claris?"

"I hope you crush it!"

CHAPTER 13

THANKFUL

Leaving Vermont was a relief.

The next couple of weeks were spent catching up on more routine cases at Amity. Cori had a number of contacts and appointments that needed responses from a counselor. Most were short-term and could be completed in a session or two. It was tricky to set up the schedule, but things fell into place rather well, and she was able to counsel several people who needed assistance for situations in their workplaces. There is a lot of hurt in the world, Cori knew, and she counted it a privilege to speak with people about relationships in and out of work that, to them, had become so problematic the individuals were thankful for the services of a trained counselor.

How ironic. What is that saying?, Cori thought. "Physician heal thyself"?

Time flew by, and it was good for Cori to be immersed

in more routine work, even if it occupied days, evenings, and some of her weekend time. She was looking forward to the Thanksgiving break and, especially, seeing Roman and Ainsleigh.

* * * * *

Cori arrived at the Briny Bluffs Resort determined to have a good time. She texted Roman when she was about a half hour away. He texted back that they were in the movie theater, but that they should be out soon after her arrival. She knew her way around, so there was no need for them to cut short their movie, she told them in a return text.

After arriving, Cori took in a deep breath. She loved being at this place. She slowly took in her surroundings. The cascading faux fall leaves, gourds, pumpkins, and cornucopia were blended into groupings, perfectly accenting the posh surroundings. The anticipation of renewed good times at the resort, as well as enjoying the place with Roman and Ainsleigh, was the best elixir she could have.

But as she was checking in, she heard a familiar voice. It took only a second to recognize who it was: Simone!

Coming around a large Christmas tree that was yet to be decorated, Simone caught a glimpse of Cori at the registration counter. Having heard Simone's voice, Cori was looking in that direction. The scowl on Simone's face quickly displayed such anger that Cori considered a run for it!

"How dare you show up here?" Simone voiced in a hushed, but extremely terse, tone.

Cori could, but often didn't, think well on her feet, and this clearly was one of those situations where it seemed any answer would net her only trouble. Should she say, "I thought you weren't coming"? and lead others to believe it was her idea to avoid Simone? Or should she say, "It's a free country"? That would be mature. She was aware there was a stunned pause and that others from Simone's family were now standing behind her. Finally, Cori said, "Roman and Ashleigh were looking for a quintessential New England Thanksgiving, and I suggested we come here." Even that wasn't the exact truth. Roman had asked to come. *Why didn't I just say that?* Cori asked herself.

Her mood plunged. Suddenly, she was disgusted with the whole situation. Not only was she furious at Simone, she seemed to compound her own problems with yet another inept response. Though she couldn't figure out the root of her problems, she could have done herself a few favors by not exploding at Simone when she was first accused of maliciously leaving Gil and Mason out of the puppet play. She knew the proverb: "A soft answer turns away wrath." If only she could put that into practice all the time!

Cori was still seized with anger when Roman and Ainsleigh appeared from the hallway leading to the theater and guest rooms. Roman hugged her with great enthusiasm, and then he spotted Simone. He released Cori after a moment and turned his attention to Simone. "Simone! I'm so glad you could make it after all! Will we all be eating dinner together?"

Simone always seemed to have her wits about her. "That would be great, Roman! But we didn't know until too late, so we had to make reservations elsewhere. It sure is good to see you and Ainsleigh. We'll have to get some time together."

How could Simone present such bold-faced lies in front of her family? Cori knew that Simone was a master at spin. It had entertained Cori often and made her uncomfortable on other occasions. Simone never seemed to be on the receiving end of deceptions, and it felt awful to realize this was the reality most of the time, Cori thought. She also thought that, until now at least, most never realized they were being duped by Simone; her charm and wit were enchanting. She now sensed that folks knew they were being "handled"—at least to a certain extent.

It was a wonderful gift to be able to make others feel good, Cori knew. Cori realized a long time ago that Simone's gift was manipulative, however, and she too had conspired to let Simone's words and actions go uncontested. She and others let themselves bask in her lavish compliments, attention, and affirmation and never challenged her sincerity.

Roman's attention turned back to Cori. "So, Sis. Where to for dinner?"

Cori, trying to act as though everything was normal, quickly responded. "I think Ainsleigh needs to experience Moody's, don't you? And let me greet my sweet sister. I'm afraid your well-deserved bear hug got lost in the chaos!"

Cori loved Ainsleigh more than she could say, and she gave her a heartfelt squeeze. Cori knew she never should overlook Ainsleigh for any reason, even the muddiest of circumstances. "Hey, girl. We're going to have such a good time. I hope you love this place as much as we do!"

"It's so special, Cori. It's something I've only seen in the movies or on Christmas cards!"

"Have you visited anything in the area yet?"

"The hotel had a shuttle to the Kittery outlets," Ainsleigh said. "It was great! I bought some L.L. Bean sandals and some gifts for folks at home."

Cori looked confused. "Hmm. Sandals. One of the last things I think about this time of year."

"And you're not from Arizona, are you, Sis?" Roman said with a chuckle.

He switched gears to Cori's dinner suggestion. "I thought Moody's was in Waldoboro. That's at least two hours from here, isn't it?"

"Yeah. I know. There's a knockoff here in town. What do you say?"

"Yeah. Let's do it."

Ainsleigh's brow furrowed a bit. She knew she was missing something.

"You'll see." Roman chuckled.

While getting ready, Cori's heart sank; she knew she had to level with Roman. She dreaded it. He was so trusting—and almost never caught up in controversy. To her, it was unexplainable how he could stay so neutral in sketchy situations.

They spent most of dinner getting caught up with the details of their lives that aren't easily covered by text, email, phone calls, or even video chats. "Tell me everything about your typical week. I want to hear it all," Cori asked them both.

Ainsleigh was quiet by nature, but it was possible for her to become animated when talking about her life passions. "Roman is so good with the kids at the children's hospital. He doesn't need to read to them, bring toys, sing, or anything that the rest of us have to 'over-plan' to be entertaining or even interesting. He has this uncanny way of just being *with them.* He lets them make suggestions, and he plays along. This can go on for hours. When we leave, they beg us to stay. Every time."

Roman shrugged his shoulders and looked like a shy school boy. "I just remember how crazy good kids are at frolicking. It's tricky in a hospital, but I just follow their lead!"

Ainsleigh shifted in her chair and looked coyly at her husband. "Roman calls it hospital horseplay hacks!"

Cori tilted her head and asked, "Do kids even know what that is?"

Roman responded with swiftness. "Oh, they get it. Don't worry about kids. Man. What sponges. They soak up everything!"

They almost glowed with happiness, and Cori's spirit rose to their level as well. She loved how invested they were in their volunteer work at the hospital's children's wing, their church, and especially in each other. They would have charmed her even if she wasn't completely partial. Her delight was somewhat marred by a foreboding about Roman, who really shouldn't be spending time in the pediatric wing of the hospital given the likely exposure to infections.

"We've been part of a sweet, small group Bible study for about four months," Ainsleigh continued. They glanced at each other, and as if on cue Ainsleigh continued. "The friendships we've formed amaze us. We've had casseroles on days they knew we had hospital treatments, folks have come by the hospital to keep us company, there's always a message reminding us of their prayers when we have a medical test, or even when we are planning activities with the kids in the hospital. Are you part of a small group, Cori? You've never mentioned it."

"Those groups are so successful in areas outside of New England, but I've never really heard that they've caught on with the churches in my area."

Cori quickly changed the subject from anything church-related. "I've forgotten what time you arrived here. Have you had a chance to walk the Marginal Way?"

"I had a hard time describing it for Ainsleigh, so we really want to, but she's been tuckered out from the trip and Kittery. We thought maybe after Thanksgiving Dinner?"

"Yeah! We'll need it!"

Dinner was long and pleasant. It just wasn't the time to bring up "the situations." *Maybe I could skip them altogether?* Cori wondered to herself.

They were about to leave when Ainsleigh said, "Uh, guys. I don't think I get it. I've been trying to figure out why this diner is so special. No offense, but I think it's rather plain. The food was good, though. And cheap."

Roman quipped, "That's it! You've hit the highlights."

Roman and Cori laughed. "That was very politic, Ainsleigh," Cori said. "Please know that we're not laughing at you. We just get a kick out of the thought of Moody's. Mom and Dad loved these 'down east' stories performed by a group called Bert and I. One of their stories is about Moody's, and it's hilarious. Plus, the word fart is used in the punchline, and Mom and Dad actually let us listen to it as kids! It was back when that was a cuss word, at least to us. That's the only time I remember that they knowingly let us listen to a cuss word!"

Roman said, "We have to play the tape. Do you still have it, Cori?"

"Yeah. Definitely. I just don't remember whether I have a tape player!"

Ainsleigh asked what should have been obvious. "What about YouTube?"

"Of course! What's wrong with us?" Cori said. "Let me take care of the bill and maybe we can play it while we relax in the Roman spa back at the resort."

They enjoyed the Roman spa, but not while listening to Bert and I. They couldn't find it on YouTube. But they had a good time invoking as many puns as they could about Roman and the spa. "It's a good thing no one else wanted to join us. For sure they would have thought we were drunk," Cori said as they took their pruned bodies from the water and retired to their rooms.

They agreed to skip breakfast so they could enjoy a one o'clock Thanksgiving dinner. It was the only reservation time available given their late decision to come. Morning coffee in the lounge area outside of the indoor pool would be all they needed in the morning. Sleeping in was perfectly acceptable.

Cori slept better than usual. She thought it must have been the relaxing time in the spa. Her condo association should look into getting one, she thought. She was able to sleep in a bit as well. She went to the lobby area at about 9 a.m. to sip and savor her first coffee of the morning. She found a spot close to the wood-burning fireplace, which had an enormous stone hearth resplendent in fall decorations. Still pumped by the enthusiasm she gained from Ainsleigh and Roman, Cori continued to soak in the wonder of this place.

Though most of the prominent areas were decked out in fall decor, Christmas decorations also were appearing. She loved the kissing balls that were lavished on posts and hanging from eaves around the grounds. Wreaths were being festooned on every door and several were hung on each of the massive windows around them. Cori enjoyed the fire. If the past patterns prevailed, the many Christmas trees would be decorated by the time they returned from Thanksgiving dinner. All of this was just as it should be.

Cori recalled that had she not been so busy at work, her home would have been partially decorated for Christmas by now. When she and Roman were living at home with their parents, the day after Thanksgiving was decorating day. During her first year on her own, she followed that pattern. But it didn't work well when she began attending the Thanksgiving retreat with Simone's family, so she slowly started hauling out Christmas decorations as soon as Halloween decorations were stored. It simply had become a necessity!

Before she knew what she was listening to, Cori was overhearing a fairly commanding voice. "Have you ever really looked into some of our Christmas traditions, or what the word Christmas really means? And you should think about most of the Christmas carols. They embellish the Bible rendition of Christ's birth in a big way!"

Cori's mouth dropped—and stayed—wide open while she gripped the arms of her easy chair. It was Simone, who was holding court just around the corner from Cori's area of the lounge, sandwiched between the lobby and the indoor pool. Had she not recognized the voice, she still would have known whose words were being spoken. She had heard most of it before. But Simone's voice usually carried a transcendent quality, as it did now.

"Here's a challenge. See who can be the first to find a reference to angels singing in the Bible." Listeners knew Simone well enough to know that, in spite of the many cultural references to angels singing, it must be that the Bible contained no clear-cut references to angels singing. Otherwise, Simone would not put out that challenge.

"One of the all-time favorite carols is 'Silent Night,'" Simone went on. "Think about it, people. Bethlehem was teeming with visitors. How silent do you think it really was? How calm? How bright is a night? Sometime, take some of the carols and focus on what an extrapolation they are. Protestants can be so critical of faith-based groups for perpetrating stories and creating traditions from actual or perceived accounts, but notice how Protestants venerate these carols and Christmas traditions year after year!"

Simone continued. Her tone was lilting and her presentation comical. People almost always were captivated by her sharp humor and magnetism.

Cori tried to be part of the woodwork and continue reading. Eventually, Simone and her followers filtered out and, finally, Roman mercifully appeared. It was so good to see him two days in a row. What a great way to start the morning! Cori asked about Ainsleigh, and he said she had been careful to get much-needed extra rest lately.

By the time their dinner reservations rolled around, they were starved. Cori didn't want to ruin their Thanksgiving dinner, but she thought it might be the best time to let Roman in on what was going on. Especially given Simone's proximity.

When they had been seated at their table and ordered, Cori did what she thought she should to get it out of the way. "I have a situation—or situations—brewing that I've been postponing telling you about, but I think I've waited long enough."

"Cori, if something is going on, why wouldn't you tell us right away?" Ainsleigh placed a supportive hand on Cori's forearm.

Cori shrugged and put down the fork she had been using to put corn relish on her cracker appetizer. "Mostly because it's such a confounded mess, and I'm not clear on what I've done to cause it!" She took a cleansing breath and then launched into the best explanation she could summon.

"Here's the upshot. I've been removed as leader of the elementary-aged youth group at church. Simone dropped the news shortly after accusing me of telling the twins—you've heard me share about them, Gus and Gil—that they were too naughty to ever touch the puppets, or something along those lines. I first noticed that I was being shunned at The Gathering, but didn't recognize what was going on until she confronted me directly. Then other things fell into place—or fell apart. It's possible Simone is the architect, but others are involved. Indications, to me, included the lack of post-event acknowledgements on The Gathering. Really, I didn't have expectations of praise or thanks, but it still was unusual for the comments to be, basically, nonexistent. I've written letters of apology, but nada. Before I knew what a pariah I had become, I asked Simone about the Briny Bluffs getaway. She told me they weren't coming this year. I was flabbergasted when I saw her here."

Roman and Ainsleigh listened quietly, both with scowls. When Cori took a breather, Roman patted her shoulder and said, "Cori, that's awful. Why didn't you tell us? Have you made any inquiries of others at church?"

"I've been too uncomfortable to go to church. Plus, I've been away so much. I asked the secretary to have Simone contact me so we can talk, but I think that ship has sailed. I still intend to talk with Pastor Lyle, but I'm so hurt and mad, I can't be confident of a good approach."

Roman just shook his head in disbelief. "This just isn't the way the church operated in the years I was a member," he said.

"I know. If I could point to any other similar incident, it might be easier to take." Cori paused, then: "Are you willing to hear one more thing?"

"Of course." Roman responded immediately, but his voice was gentle.

She then told her brother and Ainsleigh about her experience with Stewart on her second visit to Vermont. His eyes got wide, and for a moment, Cori thought he was upset with her for letting things go as far as they did that night with Stewart. When he finally spoke, he said, "Cori, are you connecting the dots here? Do you have any idea whether Simone knows Stewart?"

Whoa! Roman's sweet innocence could give way to jaded cynicism in a split-second. Cori responded: "I thought your scowl meant you were going to chide me for putting myself in a position like that with Stewart."

"Actually, for a moment I hoped there could be a romance that was going somewhere. Anything is better than nothing," Roman said.

Cori knew Roman was kidding and trying to lighten the mood for her. Quickly, she responded, "No, Roman. As mom always said, 'Nothing is better than anything.'"

CHAPTER 14

NEED TO KNOW

The time at the resort was wonderful, and Cori especially loved being there with Roman and Ainsleigh. If only there wasn't the strain of her relationship with Simone, and Simone's presence at the resort to boot! She had been praying every day for some sort of resolution to this situation.

Cori sat in her favorite chair by the fire. It was a little secluded from the rest of the lounge and lobby area. She posed as if she was reading but was actually deep in thought when Roman and Ainsleigh appeared after a brief after-dinner nap. They proposed a walk to Perkins Cove and the Marginal Way. Cori loved the idea of showing Ainsleigh where the cliffs meet the sea.

The waves put on a glorious show as the whitecaps lapped up over the craggy rocks and sprayed the promised briny mist on their chilled faces. They laughed and hurried on, anxious to get back to the toasty fireplace at the resort. "That was amazing!" Ainsleigh gushed as they headed back. Cori was thrilled her sister-in-law had enjoyed it as much as anticipated.

Just as they sat down by the fire with some densely sweet hot chocolate, Simone's party began noisily pouring into the resort. They obviously were returning home from dinner. At this point, the proximity to Simone and her family was an obvious damper to the good times Cori wished would continue for her small party. They had enjoyed things greatly so far, but she decided to ask if they could cut their time short. Cori turned to Roman and Ainsleigh. "Do you agree with me that it might be time to leave? I'm afraid any good feelings I have about being here will be further diminished if we stay much longer."

Roman and Ainsleigh both agreed.

* * * * *

Cori wasn't sure what to expect from the drive home, but Roman quickly allayed any fear of awkward silences by asking if he could bring up a delicate subject. Cori and Ainsleigh, of course, agreed, but Cori wasn't sure if she wanted to weigh down Ainsleigh any further with the unresolved issues Cori was facing. It turned out what Roman wanted to talk about wasn't related to her two issues, and Cori's thinking was quickly redirected from her situation when Roman said, "Cori, do you remember when I asked if you thought it would be OK to look into my birth family?"

"Of course. Yes. I'm so sorry I haven't asked. Do you have news?"

"Well, maybe, in a way. But can I ask a theoretical question?"

She wasn't sure what he meant, but she thought the only way to find out was to answer, "Sure."

"Two-part question, actually. Do you think it's best for someone to know they were adopted if they don't have to know? If they do know, do you think it's best for them to explore their past?"

"I would say yes to the first question. Then they would have the option of choosing whether they would want to explore their birth family. Personally, I can't imagine why they wouldn't want to know about their family of origin."

"OK. Thanks. Now I have another question. You know I started my research by looking through some files you saved from Mom and Dad's house, right? So, I was wondering whether you've looked through the boxes?"

"Not really," Cori said. "I keep meaning to go through them and do some shredding. Because of all the financial issues in settling their estate, I went through the box marked 'finances' thoroughly. I was out of energy at that point, and it seemed so noxious to face the rest. I've been putting it off in a big way, like for years."

"Oh."

"Oh what, Roman?" Cori was not at all sure where this conversation was going. Her parents were very private with her about Roman's birth circumstances. She knew he suddenly appeared in her family without a preceding pregnancy, so there was no hiding the fact to anyone that he came to them through adoption. So, what had he found out?

"Cori, did you ever wonder about how old our parents were and the details of your own birth?"

Cori tried to think. She was silent for what seemed like a long time to Roman and Ainsleigh, but they didn't push. Cory was preoccupied with scaling through her earliest memories. She tried to piece together all of those images—and carefully consider the very clear implications of the question.

As was her habit, Cori's thoughts turned inward. Had she gone through life ignoring the apprehensions she felt about her mom's glossed-over answers about her birth? Of course, she had been aware that her parents were much older than those of her peers. Another clue should have been her brother's adoption.

Perhaps she had been thrown off by her mother's stories about their family history. She told of her great-grandmother, Cora, for whom Cori was named. Cora grew up in a small town in western Massachusetts. Though tiny, the town had many villages. The cemetery where Cora was buried, and where the family visited on a couple of occasions, was on a hill overlooking the village where Cora and her sisters were raised. Cora died in her mid-thirties of pneumonia and, likely, complications related to childbirth. Her infant son died two days after she did, and they were buried together in the same casket. Cora's daughter, Cori's great-grandmother, was in her teens at the time and left to take care of the home and her younger sisters following Cora's death. The sisters already had been subjected to grief as their two-year-old baby brother had died of dysentery when they were much younger.

It was all so abjectly sad to Cori, and she had identified so closely with that part of the family tree. It never occurred to her that these strong women might not have been her real ancestors.

Finally, she spoke. Her throat was hoarse. "Would one of you be willing to drive?"

She pulled the car over at a coffee shop. They took a break, bought some beverages to go, and resumed their travel—all in silence.

Finally, Roman spoke. "Are you OK, Cori?"

"Ah, I guess. I'll be ready to talk eventually. OK?"

"Sure."

Cori felt as though she spent the rest of the trip curled up in a fetal position in the back. Symbolic, perhaps? She had prayed for a distraction from her current problems. All of this left her remembering that . . . she loved His sense of humor.

After arriving at her home, unloading, and unpacking, Cori asked Roman, "Can you show me what you found? Do you think we have the same birth parents?" She wasn't even going to try to sleep under the circumstances. At least, not right then.

Ainsleigh was quite tired from the trip. She was ready to provide support or privacy for her husband and sister-in-law. The time was right for her to retire and let them sort through their poignant past.

As they were on their way to the storage locker, Roman finally answered Cori. "There are just a couple of documents that would hint at your adoption, Cori. But there isn't anything to indicate we are biologically related. That would have been kind of nice. I haven't found out much at all about either adoption, but there was a letter I unearthed. It was a general letter asking for couples to be in contact about a prospective private adoption. It was dated two months before you were born. There was very little other evidence except for a financial statement regarding agreed upon legal and hospital fees dated about the time you were born. The files seemed purged of any other information, so I just think they missed these two."

Cori nearly grabbed the papers that Roman had pulled out, and quickly looked at them, then at him. "Sorry. This is kind of a shock, you know." She read the documents and dreaded the foreboding feeling that she could be about to go down yet another rabbit hole. She knew her tendency to become obsessed with quests that amounted to much less than this.

Her thoughts went to the person she almost always placed in front of herself. Her heart ached for him. He had his own journey to face. Trying hard to pull herself from the self-focused fixation, she forced herself to turn her attention to her brother. "How about you, Roman? What did you find out about your adoption? I can look at these later."

"As I said, I haven't found out much of anything, but I was thinking that the legal firm mentioned in the letter—obviously, about you—might lead to information about my situation. That's why I wanted your involvement, but I had to be careful about your feelings. I had no way of knowing whether this is something you want to know about yourself."

"Poor Roman. How long have you been living with this?"

"Don't worry about that. Do you need time to think, or what?"

"It's pretty whacked, finding out about this. Of course, we're going to look into it. Together. That's cool, really. I'll look at these papers and then we'll talk about what to do next. First, let's get some sleep."

Fat chance, Cori was thinking.

CHAPTER 15

WITHOUT WORDS

The day after Thanksgiving! It was the official start of the Christmas season and all the joy and promise it represented. It was the day to finish Christmas decorations: the Dickens Christmas village with its mini evergreens and all the carolers; the opaque white curtains in every window with cascading strings of mini lights; the anticipation of the tall evergreen trimmed all in white to match the icelike lights behind the billowy white curtains in the windows. Cori also loved the satellite radio stations dedicated solely to Christmas music and the wonderful decorations in every store, restaurant, and many homes, as well as the adornment of the massive town common and its gazebo.

But Cori wasn't feeling the usual elation on this late November day. In fact, she wasn't sure she could bring herself to gather the decorations from storage. She stood in a stupor at the kitchen window, simply peering at the folks who were decorating the railings of her complex. She couldn't decide whether she was sad, angry, confused, or just plain numb.

She was still caught up in her thoughts when Roman bounded through the door with coffee and Danish. He was such a good man. She needed to snap out of it. Roman had endured far more than she ever could dream, and he was so positive about life.

Moving on at least for the time being, Cori happily imbibed the eggnog-infused coffee and peppermint-frosted Danish. She was going to be happy for the season and all that it entailed. Whether looking forward or back—or maybe both ways at the same time—this was going to be fun. Roman would only be there a couple of more days, and they were going to live it up.

"Where are the decorations, Cori? Come on. Get with the season!"

"You don't want to decorate here *and* when you get back to Arizona! I don't have that much time with you. I can do all of that later."

"I love it. I want to. I'd help everybody decorate if I could. Besides, our apartment isn't that big. We won't have all that much decorating to do."

"Then we'll decorate!"

Ainsleigh appeared just then. She looked a bit confused, and her husband handed her some coffee and a Danish. "Here, hon. Everything will make more sense after your first cup of coffee."

They all laughed. Cori and Roman went to the storage locker to get the decorations while Ainsleigh enjoyed her breakfast.

By mid-afternoon they realized they hadn't stopped for lunch. They finished their last tasks of the day and admired the beauty they had created in just a few hours. Everyone got ready for an early dinner.

It was almost twilight when they arrived at the Fishing Derby restaurant. They loved seafood, and this was one of the best places within an hour's drive. They were able to take advantage of the early dinner special. Starving, they craved everything on the menu. So they each ordered a variation of the appetizer sampler and shared it all as their entree.

"I love creative dining!" Cori declared. "Remember Mom and Dad got so upset when we tried to eat off their plates? I think I have overreacted by always choosing to substitute and special-order. Sharing so many varieties of small quantities—perfection!"

The mood was jovial and the conversation almost like old times. They were about to leave when Roman asked a question. "Cori, is it OK if I stay a little longer?"

"Of course," Cori answered. "I want you both to stay as long as you can." Cori's mind raced to what fun it would be to share more of the holiday season with them and, admittedly, to what they might accomplish together in their quest for answers surrounding their births.

Ainsleigh put her hand on Cori's arm and gave her a couple of gentle pats. "That's so nice, Cori, but I need to attend to some things at home. Roman meant he would stay for a few extra days. I think this is about both of your adoptions. Is that OK, or is it too soon?"

"No, I was thinking the same thing," Cori said. "I just wish you could stay."

"I'll be fine. My parents will greet me at the airport at home. I have my fingers crossed that you quickly find out what you need to know."

Once again, Ainsleigh was combining her support with their need for privacy.

* * * * *

Roman postponed his flight for a week and borrowed Cori's car the next day to take Ainsleigh to the airport. Cori focused on some post-everything cleanup of the condo. The place hadn't recovered from the season leading up to The Gathering, and the mess entailed in decorating was heaped upon it as well.

She almost didn't hear the telephone because of the vacuum and wasn't sure how many times it had rung. Without paying attention to the caller ID, she answered and heard the voice of Reina, Della's mom. "Hi, Cori. Am I interrupting anything?"

Cori was so happy to hear from her and chuckled, "You saved me from a bad vacuuming session. I'm sorry for the number of rings you must have endured! How are you? I'm thrilled to hear from you."

"It's good to reach you. It has been so long, and Della misses you. I know it's not our business to pry, so we won't. But we are sad that you have given up the youth group and aren't attending church. If we've done something to offend you, please let us make it up to you."

What dear people, Cori thought. She was touched by their tenderness, generosity, and bravery. No one else—literally— had reached out to her in all of this time.

"Thank you for being so kind. I miss you so much, and please don't think any of this is about you." There was a brief hitch in Cori's thoughts due to the possibility that some of it . . . just might be, but she continued without hesitation. "I'm not sure if you knew I was out of town on a continued assignment and then away with family for Thanksgiving. My brother is staying with me for a week."

"Oh. I'm glad everything is OK. I won't keep you since you have company."

"He actually is driving his wife to the airport and won't be back for some time," Cori said. "He has some friends he plans to visit on the way home, so I am forced to finally clean up the mess I have let accumulate for weeks. So I have plenty of time to chat."

"Della had such a good time with you at youth group," Reina said. "She learned so much from your lessons and loved the involvement with the puppets. Meetings haven't been the same for her without you. She asks so many questions that I can't answer."

"Just because I haven't been with the group doesn't mean we can't chat. Why don't you bring her over sometime? In fact, how would now be?"

"Would you mind if I dropped her off while I do some Christmas shopping? What an opportunity to shop without prying eyes!" And then a pause. "Am I being too forward?"

"Not at all! You are so nice to check in that way. I love this plan. See you when you arrive."

Cori barely had replaced her stick vacuum on the recharger and put on her makeup when Reina and Della knocked. They all briefly embraced and chatted a bit. Reina departed, and Cori offered to show Della around. Della expressed admiration for many of the condo's trappings, and especially the Christmas decorations. Cori recalled that Della's mom was supporting them on a receptionist's salary. Cori could only think of how much pleasure it gave her to share anything she had with others, and she thanked Della again for coming to visit.

They chatted a bit since they had not gotten to know each other very well. An awkward silence led Cori to ask Della if she would like to make a bracelet, and Della readily agreed.

Cori often explained the gospel message by way of the "wordless book." "Each colorful leaf in this tiny book describes the journey of someone wanting to know God as a friend," she began. "I know it's easier to learn with your eyes, ears, and your hands together, so I also use colored beads and bracelet chords to help with understanding the message.

"I always start with the gold page and beads." As Della

placed a number of gold beads on a chord, Cori told Della about Heaven. "The book of Revelation says that the streets of Heaven are made of gold." She explained a bit about Heaven and said that many people envision living in Heaven after their life on earth is over. "In the book of Jeremiah, God says that he very much wants us there," Cori said.

Della agreed. "I hope to go to Heaven, too!"

Cori asked Della a question. "What is your opinion, Della? Most people assume that they're going to Heaven." Della expressed some doubts. She seemed to have a sense that many weren't good enough for Heaven.

"Let's take a look at the dark page." Cori then showed her a dark page and gave her several dark beads. "It is clear that God is holy, that Heaven is holy, and no wrong can take place there. The book of Romans explains that everyone is guilty of doing something wrong, and that makes the situation look hopeless."

Cori then showed Della the red page and gave her some red beads. "There was a man called Jesus, who is the same as God. God is three people in one. God the Father, God the Son, and God the Holy Spirit. It is impossible to understand, but let me try to show it this way!" Cori used three match flames to show three distinct flames, and then put them together to show one flame. They both giggled. Cori offered, "That's the best I can do."

"God sent His Son, his perfect Son, to pay for every sin that anyone has or will commit." The letter to the Hebrews, chapter 9, explains why this is necessary, Cori explained to Della.

Next, Cori showed Della an entirely clean page and gave her some clear beads. The page was flawless. John 1:12, Cori told Della, says, "But to all who receive him, who believe in his name, he gave the right to become children of God." It was as simple or as complex as one wished to make it, she explained. Cori continued, "The first step is to thank God for sending Jesus to die in our place. We ask for His forgiveness. For anyone who does that, He looks at us and sees only Jesus' perfection. He's 'got us,' as they say!"

Cori asked Della if she would like to pray that prayer, and Della said she did.

Afterward, Della said, "I have a lot of questions."

"Go for it."

"You have another page," Della said.

"We sure do. Remember I said it could be as easy or complicated as you want to make it? Well, the last color is green. Green is for growing. When we become friends with someone, it takes time and effort to really get to know them and become comfortable with them. Growing in our knowledge of God is proof that we have put our faith in Jesus. It's a relationship. We grow by reading God's Word, the Bible, praying to Him about our concerns, and meeting with others who have been covered by what Jesus did. It tells us this in the second book of Peter, chapter 3."

"Oh. That's why we go to church and youth group."

"Yes."

They had become so involved in the explanations and relevant Bible readings that all other activity had stopped. Cori asked Della if she would like to finish her bracelet while she explained as much about the wordless book as she could remember.

Della needed very little prompting to explain what she had heard as she finished her bracelet. She wrote down the accompanying Bible verses and was searching for them and reading them to Cori as Cori prepared a snack. They had just begun eating when there was a knock at the door.

Where had the time gone? Reina entered, and Della bounded toward her and tried to explain all at once what she had done. Her mom seemed surprised and curious at the same time.

"Tell her, Cori. Tell her. Mom needs to know too!"

"Della, I suggest you take some of the materials home and explain them to your mom. If you have any questions, I'll be happy to chat with you about them. I can't wait to hear how it goes."

They set up a time after school the following Wednesday. Della would come by for decorating cookies and they would continue to get to know each other.

As she closed the door after them, Cori knew everything was working out just fine in spite of her doubts. Jesus had come, He was coming again, and she loved the season that celebrated His advent as a baby.

CHAPTER 16

LEGAL EAGLES

"Roman, wouldn't you think there would have to be good signage on a massive campus like this?"

Cori felt awkward as she and Roman tried to find the right auditorium of a megachurch they had decided to attend together on Sunday. They selected a later service, which was termed contemporary. When they found the right building, and then the right auditorium, they stumbled around in the dark in what appeared to be a cavernous room. The only illumination was coming from the myriad pulsating illuminations onstage. There was equipment, and there were people, all over the stage—singing, playing, and mirroring the beat with body language. "I wonder if they will do any Christmas music?" Cori wondered aloud. She was disappointed, but not surprised, that they didn't.

After the service, some lighting was provided for folks to

safely exit. "I recognize a few people who are involved in The Gathering," Cori whispered to Roman. "Lourdes Dallas is an attorney who is somehow involved in The Gathering, though I've never really seen her doing anything." She nodded in another direction. "Over there is the baseball coach from the local high school. He offered a batting clinic this year. There are some other folks familiar to me because of food contributions and setup-takedown help, though I don't know most of their names. Still, I don't think I could be comfortable in this kind of church."

"Try not to worry, Cori. I'm hoping we can walk back the situation at our home church," Roman said. He had an appointment to talk with the pastor at Cori's church on Tuesday, so they had a plan—well, sort of a plan. Roman had been a member of the church before moving and attended for many years. He felt compelled to find out if he could determine the issue with Cori and the church. Cori, of course, had given her consent to this meeting and was considering whether to attend with him.

Cori made an effort to smile and be open to greetings from folks as they winded their way through the auditorium and campus to where their car was parked. "If I recognize folks, you'd think they'd recognize me as well," she said. "No one made the least bit of effort to welcome us."

Cori and Roman spent the afternoon exploring possible ways to research adoption information. One of the most helpful resources was the child welfare website childwelfare.gov. There they found general procedures about obtaining non-identifying information as well as identifying information, along with specific statutes for each state. They took copious notes and decided to get on the docket at the local courthouse as soon as possible.

"Monday morning will be a busy day for probate court

being the first work day after the Thanksgiving Day break," Cori said, though she knew this was conjecture on her part. She thought it might be a busy day for restraining orders needed because of family "togetherness" over the holiday.

Cori was wrong. They filled out a form with the clerk's office, and one of the friendly administrative staff left her desk and immediately took it into the court, which had yet to be called into session. "You may go in and take a seat. They should call your case soon," the woman told Cori and Roman.

Nervously, they sat near the back. It was a very old courtroom and quite ornate in its décor. The judge's bench was made of mahogany, as were the floor and door trims and paneling halfway up the walls. "Too bad it isn't maintained better. This room would be stunning if they freshened it up a bit," Cori said. "How did they have money to create such a beautiful space as this one hundred or more years ago, but we can't afford a few bucks to restore its beauty?" Roman didn't answer. He had heard these complaints from Cori before—along with her angst at the number of bridges throughout New England that were closed due to lack of funds for repairs. He thought she had a valid point. Roman suddenly realized cell phones should be turned off and pocketed his as the court officer announced, "All rise. The Probate Court of Laurel Ledge in Hartford County is now in session. Judge Robert Oceana presiding. Please be seated."

The judge read some materials, spoke with the clerk, and called their names! "Come on up to the bench," the judge said. "I see you have filed to have opened the details of your individual adoption records. According to my initial reading of the petition, I agree that the process may commence. Please see the clerk at the break for the decree."

And that seemed to be it! They agreed later that the ease in which the judge ordered the release of original birth certificates to both probably was because of Roman's medical needs.

Already they had discussed how odd it had been of their parents not to have provided Roman with medical histories of his birth family.

They went back to the clerk's office at the session break. The same assistant told them to have a seat and the clerk would call them when she had a moment. They had just settled in when she stepped behind the counter and called their names. She didn't call them into her office, but spoke in a hushed tone. "The judge was about as radical in moving forward as I've ever seen, but he wanted me to be somewhat cautious in the event partial information was under special protection. So, he has decided to appoint an intermediary to do the first round of research. The intermediary is not required in this state, but the judge is trying to combine expediency and caution."

Cori and Roman signed the necessary paperwork. The administrative assistant said they would be contacted soon with the identified intermediary; likely, she said, this would be a local attorney.

"So, I guess that's all for now?" This was Roman's way of checking in with Cori, and he said it as they were descending the massive concrete steps that reminded him of the Manhattan Public Library steps.

"I guess," Cori said. "I had no idea things would move so quickly. I wouldn't doubt that his concern for your family of origin and medical history prompted him to action. Mom and Dad were really wrong not to have given you the information you needed long before they died. Anyway, there's no going back. How about a quick bite at the Sandwich Club?"

The stranger she had seen a few weeks before really wasn't on her mind when she suggested lunching there, but she thought about him later and was disappointed he hadn't made a showing. She thought about how silly she was for letting her mind wander and thinking that as well!

"Cori, let's go by the law firm in Hartford that was on the letterhead of the letter Mom had hidden in her Bible," Roman suggested.

"Oh, things aren't moving fast enough for you, Roman?" Cori teased. "I thought I was the one to act now, think later!"

He patted her head, which she hated. "I've been thinking about this a long time, Cori."

"Point taken."

There was a lobby area where an administrative assistant served as a receptionist for all the other receptionists in specialty areas. He was quite condescending and his tone was affected by a highfalutin accent, or so Cori thought. They showed him the letter, and he made a copy of it and returned the letter to them. "Since you have no appointment, you will need to have a seat in the waiting area here," the man said.

"Of course. A seat in the 'outer sanctum,'" Cori said under her breath to Roman as they dutifully took a seat.

The first few minutes of the wait Cori spent trying to take in the splendor of the place. It wasn't just the ample Christmas decorations. The rococo style reminded Cori a bit of the lobby to the Boston Opera House. The grand staircases, cascading upward on either side of the receptionist counter, solidified the comparison. It was out of place in this cosmopolitan area, but interesting.

With her jaw drop back under control, Cori started to rifle through coffee table books reporting on various aspects of the firm. Pictures of partners, associates, clerks, and support staff were included. Cori recognized Lourdes Dallas from the church they had attended the day before. It came back to her that Simone had mentioned more than once that Lourdes was quite a high-powered attorney. "Roman. Look. The caption under the picture of Lourdes Dallas gives her middle name as the same as the last name of the attorney who signed the letter pertaining to what we assume is my adoption. The attorney who signed it is now listed as a deceased founder of the firm. Lourdes probably is in her early sixties. This picture in his memory looks very much as a well-preserved eighty-five-year-old would appear. I'll bet he was Lourdes's father. Maybe Lourdes can help us."

Then a pause. "Speak of the devil," she whispered as she nudged Roman just as Lourdes descended one of the opulent staircases with an individual who likely was a colleague. Cori sat up straight while considering whether to initiate a conversation. She decided the two were too absorbed in their tête-à-tête to interrupt—but Cori was certain Lourdes noticed her. Not very subtly, she turned to her colleague and proceeded out the door. It seemed almost as though she had done so abruptly, as in a huff. "Well, I've gotten a belly full of cold shoulder lately, though I'm still pretty foggy on the why," Cori said to her brother. "You did notice the snub, right?"

Roman wasn't nearly as sensitive to these gestures as Cori, but he agreed. "Yeah. That was pretty good theater."

They had been waiting a long time when a young woman in business attire approached where they were seated. "Are you the individuals who have inquired about adoption records? I called the probate clerk's office in Laurel Ledge, and an intermediary already has been named." The attorney was located in Laurel Ledge, and the clerk handed them a piece of paper. Cori recognized the name of the firm.

They thanked her and decided to stop by on their way home to make an appointment. Entering the small firm was a very different experience from that of Lourdes's. Its humble receptionist area was contiguous with three attorneys' offices, all with names on the doors visible from the waiting area. They apologized to the receptionist for not having an appointment and gave a brief overview of their quest, along with the name of the attorney provided earlier.

The receptionist asked them to make themselves comfortable and disappeared. She returned with a professionally dressed, middle-aged woman. She introduced herself. "I'm Ardis Thompson. Please call me Ardis." She invited them into her office and they began things with some small talk.

Eventually, the conversation shifted to the reason Cori and Roman were there. Ardis explained some of what they already knew. "Often the research on adoption proceedings can take considerable time and is not always successful in obtaining the desired information. However, in Roman's case, I was able to find out very quickly that his adoption was filed with a mutual consent registry. This meant that the information was there and could be revealed any time after age twenty-one. I'm surprised, Roman, that your parents haven't shared this information with you. Are they still living, by the way?"

"No. They've been deceased for almost eight years. They were very open about the fact that I was adopted, but they never offered any information beyond that."

"Well, I think your wait is nearly over. I could have information for you by late in the day tomorrow. I might not have official documents, but I am authorized by the court order to reveal information verbally and follow up later with written documentation."

Roman held his breath for a split-second, then smiled broadly. "Thank you. Now that I'm close, I can hardly wait!"

Cori's heart melted. Roman was kind and thoughtful, but seldom would she describe him as emotional. She didn't blame him. She was glad for him.

"Cori, I promise I will begin the process soon for you as well. I sense there will be more research required than in Roman's case. With any luck, I hope to have some initial information the next time I speak with Roman."

"Thank you. Really. We had no idea we could see you today. We're very grateful." Roman shook her hand, and he and Cori left.

"Let's not eat out again," Cori said as they headed out. "I have a good recipe for pasta carbonara. It's quick, not too hard, and doesn't require many ingredients."

They worked together in the kitchen, chatting the whole time, and during the meal as well.

It was late when they decided to watch some made-for-television Christmas movies. Roman did not have the same affinity for this form of entertainment as Cori, but he tolerated them well because, over the years, he had no choice.

Just before turning in, Roman ventured a question. "Should we do anything to prepare for our meeting with Pastor Lyle tomorrow?"

Cori yawned, put her hand over her mouth, and apologized. "Yeah. We probably should. I don't think this is going to be easy. Where do we start?"

Neither said anything. "I should have thought of it earlier. I'm too tired to think, but we're simply after information," Roman said. "How hard can it be? I'm willing to just listen, if that's what it takes." He was such an optimist.

"I'm not so sure, but I've got nothing right now. See you in the morning, little brother."

As she tried to sleep, Cori remembered the letter she had sent not long ago as an apology to Eugenia, mother of Mason and Gil. It was heartfelt and truly left the door open for a continued relationship. She had included individual letters to Mason and Gil to let them know they were unique and valued for their participation in any of the ministries, including the puppet plays.

She hadn't included any "you messages," though she could have. The apology was written without qualification. She included no excuses and took upon herself full responsibility. She hadn't received a reply, but she kept a copy to take with her to the meeting the next day.

CHAPTER 17

"To the Church at Ephesus"*

Cori and Roman arrived on time for the meeting at the church offices. They greeted Cindy. "Hello, Cori. Hi, Roman. Go ahead and have a seat." Cindy's tone wasn't all that cordial, and her avoidance of further discussion or contact was similar to someone who suspected her guests had the flu or something worse.

Pastor Lyle obviously wasn't on the premises and bounded through the side door to the reception area about ten minutes after their scheduled time. Without making eye contact, he said, "Hi, Roman. Hi, Cori. Come on in to my office."

---

* Reference to Revelation, chapter 2, regarding the church at Ephesus. In spite of their generous works, they had left their First Love.

Cori and Roman each chose a seat without further instructions from Pastor Lyle, who was hanging up his coat. He then proceeded to his desk and began shuffling around some papers without taking a seat. Eventually, he looked at Roman. "How are you and Ainsleigh doing? I hope the Arizona sun is better for your lungs."

"We're doing well, Pastor. How is your family?" Roman stayed cordial, but didn't sense there was any genuine interest in he and Ainsleigh on the part of the pastor, so he stopped short of offering any details.

"Oh, they're fine. Busy with activities, no matter what time of year."

Pastor Lyle took a deep breath. "Cori, just what are your intentions toward the church?"

She didn't want to bungle another opportunity to respond appropriately, so she took a moment to collect her thoughts. Then she turned the question around and offered it back to him. "I guess the question is, what are the intentions of the church toward me?"

Pastor Lyle immediately put on his preacher hat. "Well, young lady. Church attendance is commanded in the Bible. Not only are we to attend, decisions by church elders are final. We also should talk about exhibiting proper temperament, especially when dealing with young children. The church has the power to terminate memberships when folks are ill-prepared to participate effectively within the body."

Cori wanted to handle this interview productively, but she quickly became enraged.

She maintained composure long enough to speak, even though she wasn't sure she had any voice, literally or figuratively. "I see I have made a mistake. This was to be Roman's appointment. Please excuse me. Roman, I'll leave you the car and I'll take a cab. See you at home." She quickly handed Roman the car keys and calmly left.

Once outside, she called a cab.

She found it extremely hard to stop fuming. She also realized how long it had been since she had connected with anyone familiar to her, except for Roman and Ainsleigh. She hadn't had a real conversation with Byron or Jessalyn in so long. There certainly were others she could talk with, and she knew she had to do something to maintain her footing. So far, she was holding it together.

"It's all an act." She said this out loud to herself in the back of the cab!

Next, with her cell, she decided to try Jessalyn. She was hoping Jessalyn could help her make sense of what was happening with church.

Jessalyn answered on the first ring. "Hey, Cori. How are you? I'm so glad you called. I went by your apartment a couple of times, but I haven't found you home."

"What a relief. I haven't found many folks who are willing even to look me in the eye, say anything of talking to me!"

"Oh no. Is it really that bad?"

"I think so. I just had a meeting with Pastor Lyle and ended up walking out. Roman stayed, so I'll see if he has found out anything when he comes back."

"I think I should come over so we can talk in person."

"Sure. I'm in the back of a cab right now, but I'm about to arrive home. Anytime is good."

Roman and Jessalyn arrived at nearly the same time. They were well acquainted, and they all made some lunch together while getting caught up on Roman's news. Jessalyn was especially understanding of Roman and Ainsleigh because of her medical knowledge.

They made themselves comfortable in the living room with some Christmas cupcakes Jessalyn brought from the Sandwich Club. "What is your time constraint, Jessalyn?" Cori asked.

"Oh, I'm good. My shift doesn't start until 7 p.m. Everybody at home has commitments after school, so their dad's going to be the chef and chauffer today."

First they filled her in on their most recent distraction—the adoptions. "Wow! I never knew that you were adopted, Cori," Jessalyn said. "Your family came to the church when you were a tiny baby. It was just about the time I could help in the baby nursery, and I remember the thrill of there being a newborn. Of course, all of us remember Roman's adoption. By then, we had known your family for several years."

They told her what had been accomplished so far. Cori also mentioned what seemed to be the larger firm's involvement, which seemed shadowy, and the snubbing she received from Lourdes when they were there to inquire.

Cori also told Jessalyn a little about the situation at church, at least from Cori's point of view.

"Is this a good segue for you to hear about the balance of the Pastor Lyle debacle?" Roman asked, believing this likely was an appropriate time to jump in.

"Uh oh. It doesn't sound as though it went very well," Cori said.

"Ah." Roman accompanied his remark with a hand gesture that emphasized how worthless the meeting became. "It was just more of the same. Pastor Lyle puked out platitudes that were meaningless under the circumstances and added a thinly veiled suggestion that you should continue attending elsewhere. He knows where we attended church on Sunday. He had the nerve to drag out your letter of apology and quoted from it to reinforce your guilt." Once again, Roman gave a hand gesture that essentially said, "To heck with it."

"So, what did you do?" Cori was curious how they parted.

"I finally cut him off. I said, 'With no respect due, Pastor, you have treated my sister so as to preclude any knowledge that she wasn't born yesterday, sat under biblical teaching for a lifetime, spent many years teaching the Bible to children, and is in the counseling profession to boot. I perceive my sister simply is a target, and there is nothing going on that warrants this treatment of her.'

"Then I just walked out. I didn't even say good-bye."

Cori hardly could believe what she was hearing. Knowing that eventually Roman would crash, she tried to provide comfort by gently patting his arm. "I really appreciate your support. I hope you'll be OK," she said. She simply couldn't believe what a kick-butt her brother could be in support of her. But, she added, "I'm a little worried you might feel a measure of remorse for going off script in such a big way."

"There's a time to be angry. I'm not a chump, and I won't sit by and let him serve up this crap. I'll be careful not to hold on to the anger. I know the dangers."

"Paul's letter to the Ephesians, right? Thanks, Bud."

Cori went on to another thought. "I guess I'm not surprised, but Pastor Lyle's possession of my letter leads me to conclude that there is some collusion going on."

"I don't doubt it, now that I have a better idea of what's been happening," Jessalyn said, joining the conversation. "I dropped by the church office Monday to leave some supplies for the health clinic. Though it was his day off, Pastor Lyle's car was there. I also saw Simone, Lourdes, and Eugenia arrive together and walk into the pastor's office."

"Wow! 'Family meeting,' huh?" Cori quipped.

"Seems so," Jessalyn replied. "I'm not impressed with whatever strategy they thought they came up with, but it's definite what their goal was. But why, Cori?"

"Why *anything*? What do they have against me, and what has Lourdes to do with it?" Cori was incredulous.

"All I know is that Simone worships Lourdes. She would do anything for her," Jessalyn said.

"What do you know about Lourdes?" Cori asked.

"OK. We're deep into gossip and speculation at this point,

but I think your situation warrants some disclosures and brainstorming. Besides his practice, Dr. Dallas served as the executive director and attending physician for the nearby shelter for pregnant women, Compass Points. I volunteered there a few evenings a month for about six months during the time I was studying for my nursing degree."

Cori mumbled softly. "Compass Points, again."

"What?"

"Never mind right now. Please, go on, Jessalyn."

"I was very uncomfortable around Dr. Dallas and his familiarity with other female staff members and residents. I never observed anything overt, but it was enough for me to give up volunteering. I freely acknowledge I am more sensitive to that kind of behavior than most, but only a few people I talked with hadn't noticed that something was awry. Now maybe, perhaps, it wasn't. But if it was, no one was addressing it that I can tell."

CHAPTER 18

CONNECTIONS— OLD AND NEW

"Where has the time gone?" Roman was the first to notice. "Excuse me. I want to call Ardis, the attorney, on the chance she has found out something about my adoption."

He left Cori and Jessalyn in the living room and went to the guest room to make the call.

Ardis came on the line very quickly. "Hi, Roman. I'm glad you called. I have some news, but I need you to prepare yourself for some disappointment."

Roman just wanted to get to it. "Yeah. OK. What's up?"

"I'm sorry that this is part of the news, but neither of your parents is alive. Adoption was grandma's decision as the closest living relative. She is still living. I was able to contact her directly, and she is eager to meet you. She lives in the

Adirondack region of New York, and I will forward all of the information to you by courier first thing in the morning.

"Roman, truly I am very sorry. I can't imagine how hard it is for discovery and loss to happen all at once. Is your sister there for support?"

Roman had to clear his throat before answering. "Yes." Recovering his almost-always courteous demeanor, he said, "Thank you so much."

"Very quickly let me add this," Ardis said. "Please let your sister know I have made no progress for her as yet. I'll be in touch as soon as I have news."

"Yes. I'll let her know."

Roman returned to Cori and Jessalyn, the three of them forming a small group of sorts that had become quite intimate in the last couple of hours. He quickly let the two women know all he had been told; he received their undivided attention while he told them. Their support was complete. Both provided acknowledgement for who he was as an individual and promised to be by his side throughout his upcoming journey.

Eventually the time came for Jessalyn to leave, and goodbyes were said along with reassurances of support.

After Jessalyn left, Cori and Roman debriefed for a long time. Roman needed to have a private video chat with Ainsleigh in the guest room, and Cori turned on the DVR to see if it had a good Christmas movie in store. She needed something interesting and mindless at the same time—whatever that meant. Embrace the ambiguity, she always said.

Nothing new was there, so she accessed the perpetual play list of Christmas movies she retained throughout the year. She loved *Home by Christmas* and was in the perfect mood to watch one of her favorite stories about coping after the loss of just about everything. It was the story of a former middle-class housewife and how, as a homeless divorcee, she substituted free services for formerly expensive commodities. It was, to Cori, a terrific recounting of the hope she needed right now. She was at the point in the movie when the heroine was preparing for her daughter to come home for Christmas when Roman emerged from the next room. He looked drained. Cori paused the movie and waited for him to speak.

"Ainsleigh wants to come back immediately and go with me to meet my grandma." Roman took a deep breath and sat beside her.

Cori rubbed his arm. "I'm so sorry you won't get to meet your parents. I'm amazed you can put one foot in front of the other, Roman. Feel free to disintegrate at any time, and I'm serious. This is too much all at once."

Roman stood and paced a bit, but managed a smile. "I don't think I need to fall apart. Really. I'm doing OK. I just need to process it all, and I'm not going to lose sight of all the good that has happened." He turned and looked straight at Cori. He put his hands in his pockets and shrugged. "I had parents who loved me, and I have a sister who would do anything for me. I lost parents as an infant, but I didn't have to find out about it until adulthood. I have to say that things could be a lot worse.

"Ainsleigh and I are going to make arrangements to meet my grandma as soon as she arrives." He looked a bit sheepish, and his words belied his real emotions. "What an adventure, huh?"

Cori felt helpless on how to help her brother. "Roman, I can't wait to meet your grandma, and I will as soon as you say the time is right."

"Got it, Sis."

"Oh, and go ahead and use my car when you need it. I have a rental coupon that I never thought I'd need to use. I'm going to go ahead and use it."

"I could rent a car if you would prefer," Roman said, telling Cori he thought it might be a better idea for insurance and all things involved. They both agreed.

"So, what are you watching?" he asked.

"I think you've seen this one before." She gave him a brief description to remind him.

"Oh yeah. I remember. I can join it in progress." He wasn't really listening anyway. He was deep in thought as the movie played and they munched on popcorn and sipped hot chocolate.

When the movie finished, they said goodnight. What an exhausting day it had been. Once again, neither knew what kind of night it would be.

* * * * *

Cori knew that Jessalyn's shift wasn't over until 7 a.m., and then she would be ready for some sleep. So she decided to wait until afternoon before filling her in on Roman's plan. She was thankful that Roman was getting some sleep after all. She looked forward to her get-together in the afternoon with Della and began preparations for making Christmas cookies.

Roman awakened to the smell of coffee and emerged in a bit of a stupor. "Hey, Sis. The coffee smells great. Can you tell I need it?"

"It shows!" She smiled.

"Ainsleigh texted late last night that she will arrive soon after lunch. She'll be tired, but we want to set up a meeting if we can get with my grandma tomorrow. I'll pick Ainsleigh up at the airport and drive straight to the Adirondacks. We can spend the night there."

"I understand the need to get answers right away, but how are you really feeling about meeting the person who gave you away?" Cori asked. "I know that sounds insensitive, but I don't have great feelings about that particular person in my life, whoever it is."

"The sooner I meet her, the sooner I find out what kind of person she is. I can withhold judgment until then."

"Of course you can. There's a lot you can do that I can't seem to."

"I reserved a rental. Would you be able to drop me off?"

"Of course."

"Cori, something else occurred to me last night. My first call about my adoption was to the big, opulent law firm. It was such an innocuous call that I almost forgot about it. They dismissed my question out of hand, saying nothing could be accomplished on the phone. But what occurred to me was that my phone call was just about the time you started having problems at church. I'm getting a little paranoid about Lourdes Dallas's involvement in all of this."

Cori wasn't thinking straight due to the overload of information. "Why did you call them again?"

"As soon as we considered coming for Thanksgiving, I thought I would try to get some leads and follow up while we were here. Since I got nowhere, I dropped the idea for the time being. Then, you know, I decided to stay and everything started falling into place . . . or should we say, fall apart?"

Cori had to laugh. What else could one do? "Let me give that some thought, Roman." She hadn't shared with Roman or Jessalyn what she now suspected about the Dallases and Della. She had to think about it carefully before doing anything that could negatively impact Della. It was interesting that Roman picked up on the timing issue with Lourdes, but she was convinced it all had to do with Reina and Della.

By the time they were ready to leave the house, they were confident Ardis's firm would be open for business and placed the call on the way. When they arrived to pick up the materials, Ardis asked to see them. Before they were seated, Cori thanked Ardis for moving so quickly. Ardis acknowledged that initial work already had begun based on Roman's call to the other firm.

"Isn't there a confidentiality issue?" Cori was stunned.

"I can't go into details, but there was some sharing of duties with regard to Roman's adoption that involved both firms. But the details resided with us, and we were prepared for Roman's inquiry as soon as the contact with us was formal."

That explained a lot. Cori and Roman thanked Ardis, and they moved on.

They easily obtained a fuel-efficient but safe car for Roman and Ainsleigh. They said their good-byes, and Roman went directly to the airport. Cori left and spent some time shopping for supplies that were so badly depleted due to her lack of attention the last few weeks.

It was nearly lunchtime when she left the last store on her list, and she decided to drop by the Sandwich Club. The suspense she earlier felt about possibly seeing the stranger had waned due to a lack of success. But she still savored the brief but delicious feeling of a possible eye-lock with him.

Byron was at the Sandwich Club lunching alone, and she summoned up the courage to approach him. She really missed him.

"Hey, Byron. How are you?"

"Hey. I've been meaning to be in touch with you. It's been a long time. How's it going?"

Cori couldn't decide whether to ignore the truth, gloss over the truth, or give the socially expected response that all was well.

Middle ground? Why not? "I'm really fine, but sometime when you can stomach the pain, I'll top any drama you've endured from me in the past."

"I'm working on paperwork and have all the time in the world for lunch. I'm all ears. In fact, I need to apologize about the Stowe-area case. I was a jerk and you were right to pursue it. I should have been there to support you."

"Thanks. Probably just pregnancy hormones," she joked. "I'm still waiting to see what else they find out, if anything."

Byron continued. "I didn't listen to you about the crap that was going on with your church, either. I am sorry."

"OK, thanks. That means a lot, Byron."

"Can I explain?"

"Sure."

"So many people I have known who have pushed for justice in a given situation have simply been dismissed out of hand—at best. At worst, the justice seekers are harmed in the process. I've given up trying. Besides, I knew how much you doted on Simone, and I always tried to respect your relationship. But I have been uncomfortable with her since we first became acquainted. Look, I'll try not to judge based on my intuition."

"That never stopped me!" Cori interrupted. They both laughed. "Go ahead, intuit!"

Byron continued. "You do know she wants to be the youth pastor of a huge church? She's going to climb that ladder no matter what. She's skillful at it, and she garners anyone for followers that she can. If she has to choose between loyalties, she's gonna go with the one that has the most to offer her ambitions—and to heck with any that don't."

Cori had observed from Simone's plethora of tweets that she had quite a following and was masterful in the way she could curry favor from her followers. Eventually, it was hard for Cori not to gag, so she finally unfollowed her . . .

She found her thoughts returning to Byron.

"So, she's targeting me in order to suck up to someone else?"

"Oh yeah."

"Is that why you said, 'What did you really expect, Cori?'"

"Yeah. Sorry."

"It hurt. A lot. For a long time."

"I don't know what to say. I really am sorry."

"OK. I'm just glad you're back."

"I am. And I am too."

After a pause, Byron continued. "Anyway, I think you have more to tell me, right?"

She didn't shorten the adoption stories by a single detail. She leveled it all. Byron was appropriately stunned. Because she had been so detailed, when he regained his composure after the initial shock, he said, "What a minute. You mentioned Lourdes Dallas. What did I tell you?"

"I can't figure out why, though," Cori said. She thought it was OK to feign ignorance for the time being. Once again, she wanted to keep Della out of this.

"She and her ilk are why I stopped attending mainline churches," Byron said. "Simone, too, as a matter of fact. As I said, she's a user. So, let's see. Megachurch . . . moneyed, perfectionist, influential broad . . . . Simone's ambitions . . . I don't know. How dull would we be if we couldn't connect those dots?"

Cori laughed and said, as if singing, "Byron is venting."

He put his head down and chuckled.

She knew it was best to draw this part of the conversation to a close, but she couldn't help but be curious about Byron's perceptions of Lourdes. So she went on.

"I know you will take what I'm about to say within the context of what you know about me. But if Lourdes gravitates toward power, why has she always dismissed me out of hand long before any of these recent events occurred? She's remotely involved in The Gathering," Cori added, tersely. "Though how, I don't know. I've never seen her actually doing anything. But anyway, why have I always sensed that I was a nobody around her? I'm in charge of the whole thing!"

"Cori, Cori, Cori," Byron began. "You're a student of human behavior, and I still have to explain so much to you! There are so many obvious answers to your question. To begin, you aren't a glory hound. I know that and so does everybody else. The Gathering is a great event. But its mission is humble and it serves those in need. She's involved only to the point where she can burnish her image with the folks who matter. That's the impetus for practically all her efforts. Whoever coordinates the effort is immaterial—unless that person has some other inherent value to her."

She really didn't know why she had mentioned Lourdes, since it wasn't all that germane to explaining recent events to him. So she decided to shift away from that angle. "I get it. Byron, you haven't told me: how is Cheri and the pregnancy?" She was convinced of his simpatico, and she really did want to find out about Cheri.

"Just fine. Thanks for asking. They found out that the baby is due sooner than we thought." A pause. "Uh, Cori?"

"Yes?"

"If I didn't know you were a person of faith, I would have told you about Him a long time ago, you know."

"OK. Thanks."

Cori knew she should have clarified the subject of Byron's faith a long time ago. As a Christian, it's what you should do.

CHAPTER 19

LOVE STORY

Roman couldn't help but worry about Ainsleigh and the impact all this traveling and emotional upheaval might have on her health. He prayed about every aspect of the developments in his, Ainsleigh's, and Cori's lives, and trusted he could pull the plug on all of the activity if at any point it proved detrimental to his loved ones.

As soon as Ainsleigh came through the plane exit gate, they embraced and held each other for a long time. "No matter how many distractions I may have or how intense they are, nothing can keep me from missing the love of my life, Ainsleigh," he said softly to her. "As important as these answers about my family are to me, we'll drop it all and return home for the sake of your health. I love that you're with me for this adventure, but you have to be honest with me about how you're feeling."

Ainsleigh was overjoyed to see him as well, to say the least.

"Roman, I want to experience this with you. This is so exciting for me, and I don't want you to be alone. I'll rest all I can, but the important thing is for me to be with you."

They collected her luggage and immediately set out for the inn where Roman secured reservations for the next couple of nights. He told Ainsleigh about the inn and his initial chat with his grandmother.

Ardis had disclosed that his grandmother resided in a small complex of assisted living apartments near Schroon Lake. She provided the telephone number and indicated she had been able to get through to his grandmother, Helen, on the first try. Ardis had prepared Helen for his call without revealing a great deal of information. She was able to let Roman know that Helen was at once shocked and thrilled to hear he would be in touch.

Roman, too, had made contact on the first try. He recounted the conversation to Ainsleigh. "I think she struggled to talk through her tears. She said she assumed I was dead, but I didn't ask her what made her think that," Roman said. "I kept the conversation short. It's cute that she gave me directions to her place. I don't think most folks in her generation are comfortable or even familiar with GPS. But anyway, maybe it was a good idea given that we're already in the boondocks."

After more than two hours of driving, they started to notice snow on the ground. After a few more minutes went by, the snow became significant. Ainsleigh only had seen snow a couple of times while staying with Cori, but never had there been this much accumulation. "Roman, is this what they mean by a winter wonderland?" she said. "It's beautiful. Look at it on the trees and everywhere!" For the first time since being seated in the car, she let go of his hand and focused all her attention on the trees sparkling in the sunlight, the excitement of the snow-crusted road, and the perceived safety the tall snowbanks provided on either side of the road.

As they approached their destination, Ainsleigh said, "Oh, Roman. The inn is absolutely lovely." As they walked the steps to the inn, Ainsleigh turned. "Look at the ice-covered lake! They've cleared it of snow for the skaters." Ainsleigh was mesmerized and watched from inside the lobby as the hardy skaters on the lighted portion of the lake frolicked, danced, performed tricks and, in some cases, barely stood upright. Roman went to the counter to check in. He spotted a beautiful dinner buffet in the restaurant just off the lobby and returned to tell Ainsleigh.

They followed the bellhop to their room and began to settle in. "I can't believe we've been able to enjoy two vintage inns within a week's time, Roman. This is beautiful. It's very different from the Maine coast, though. Most of the decorations in Maine used evergreens. These decorations are all Victorian, and they match the décor of the inn perfectly." Ainsleigh never saw Victorian décor in Phoenix! The tree in the lobby had small faux scrolls with Christmas carols printed on them. Instead of ribbon there was long, wending parchment paper with ancient scribing printed on it. There were ribbon eyelet angels all over it, and Victorian ladies' fans, dress boots, and hats—all in maroon. They had mini old-fashioned ice skates, beaded silk-covered ornaments, and lights that look like real candles. Every shelf, cabinet, and available floor space had painted wooden angels, snowmen, Father Christmas. Ainsleigh was enjoying it all.

In spite of her enthusiasm, Ainsleigh was tired. "I'm going to rest just a bit. If you'll wake me for the buffet, please."

Later, at dinner, the flames from the fireplace created a beautiful visual backdrop as well as an audible one, with its crackling sound of hardwood logs. It was so different from desert décor, which she loved. "This is such a special place, Roman. I'm loving every minute of it." Ainsleigh ate well at first, but quickly turned to only picking at her food.

Roman noticed, as he always did. "I don't think that short rest was quite enough, Babe. Let's finish up so you can get some rest."

"Roman, it's beautiful here and there's so much to see. You don't have to come upstairs yet. Stay and enjoy the scene here and your food, OK?"

"Are you sure?"

"Of course. I don't think spouses should be a ball and chain for heaven's sake!"

When Roman had finished overeating, he telephoned Cori, who was anxious to hear from him. He filled her in on the trip thus far, the beauty of the inn and its surroundings, and his concern for Ainsleigh. For the first time, he told Cori his thoughts that he would drop all of this and fly back to Arizona if his concerns for Ainsleigh's health increased even an iota. He was emphatic in telling her so.

When he returned, Ainsleigh hadn't slept yet. They had a Bible reading together and a time of prayer, and then she retired. Thankfully, she dropped off to sleep rather quickly. He could tell this from her measured, slightly labored breathing. And though this pattern represented the biggest struggle in her life, he loved the familiar sound and the comfort it brought him—because it belonged to her.

Roman spent some time reflecting on the questions he had lived with for so long. *Do I look like Helen? Will she know about my father? Will she have pictures? Will I even like her? Will she even like me?* He already suspected she harbored no resentment toward him or his appearing in her life, and that relief was as important as answers to any of his other questions.

* * * * *

There was no outside access to the apartments in which Helen lived, and Roman was relieved there was security at the only visitor entrance. The front desk attendant called her apartment and received her permission to send her company on. Roman and Ainsleigh found Helen's apartment with no trouble.

He knocked, and Helen answered promptly. Her attempts at restraint in her greeting were obvious. She almost froze in place except for her hands, which went up to her mouth and kept her mouth hidden. Eventually, she offered her hand. When Roman reached for it, she grabbed it with both of her hands. Roman asked, "Is a hug OK?" At that point, she grabbed him and held on as if making up for the past twenty-five years. Eventually, he remembered to introduce Ainsleigh.

"Uh . . . obviously, I'm Roman. This is my wife, Ainsleigh."

"I thought this day would never come," Helen said. She cried for a second, then recovered quickly and said, "Please. Come in. Come in."

Her studio apartment was crowded with pictures. She sat down briefly, but swiftly rose again. "May I tell you about your family and show you the pictures?"

Roman was anxious and could only muster one word in response. "Please!"

Helen pulled out the first photo. "This is you when you were first born. This is you with your mom, my daughter. Her name was Ruby."

Roman froze as he looked at the picture. It was surreal. It had to be a dream. He couldn't let himself succumb to the emotions nearing the surface. He had to change focus, and Helen was prepared to move on if he was.

"Here are some pictures of your mom when she was a girl." He and Ainsleigh pored over them. Ruby was so childlike in all the pictures. And there was something else about most of the pictures that was painfully obvious.

"I only see a few pictures of Ruby without oxygen. Did she have cystic fibrosis, too?"

"Yes. She was born with the same lung disease you have. In

this area, back then, the doctors didn't offer much in the way of knowledge about how to treat cystic fibrosis. Ruby spent more time in the hospital than not. I lost my husband when she was a teenager, and I used his life insurance money to take her to Hartford, Connecticut, where there was an experimental treatment program. We had high hopes that she would get better. I think she improved a little, and we decided to stay to spend the entire year called for by the program.

"It was her last year of high school, and she was determined to finish high school and the medical study in the same year if she possibly could. A young student from a nearby community college volunteered to help tutor the kids who were in the hospital. Lewis took a special shine to Ruby, and she to him. They became inseparable.

"Ruby and Lewis were unrealistic about her progress. That was partly my fault. I hadn't told her that doctors told me her life expectancy would be very few years past twenty. Anyway, in a strongminded move, Ruby and Lewis eloped to New York City. They were in touch almost immediately, but I was still sick with worry. We tried to find them, but I didn't have much for help or resources.

"They hadn't thought this through, obviously. After a couple of weeks they ran out of money, and Ruby was very weak without her treatments. They had no choice but to return. Of course, Ruby had to be hospitalized immediately. Instead of improving after her return, she slowly seemed to get worse. Then we came to understand that you were on the way, Roman!

"Ruby made it through the pregnancy and delivery. Because of her hospitalization, you were diagnosed very quickly and received the best care, I believe, anyone could." Helen stopped for a moment and dried her eyes.

She continued after a short rest. "You and Lewis were the two best joys of her life. I've never seen her so happy. I can honestly say, I wouldn't change either if I had to go back."

Helen was now quietly sobbing.

Roman moved to her and gave her a side hug. He started to say they could take a break, but Helen continued through her tears.

"Sadly, her decline continued, as expected. They were able to keep her comfortable, but she passed away when you were about three weeks old."

In their own ways, all three were crying. Roman showed it the least, as one might expect. He distracted himself by continuing with the pictures while Helen and Ainsleigh pulled themselves together and rejoined him.

"Your dad loved you so much, Roman. Did you see the picture of him holding you?"

Helen found the picture and handed it to him. "Ainsleigh," Roman said, "are you seeing what I'm seeing?"

Ainsleigh could hardly see through her tears, but took the picture and looked at it. Even through her tears she could plainly see the resemblance of the adult Roman to Lewis.

"Yes, Roman. You look so much like him. I almost declared it as soon as I opened the door," Helen said, smiling. She was no longer as teary and seemed ready to continue.

"When Lewis met Ruby, he was severely depressed and under the care of a doctor. The doctor suggested that Lewis do something to give to others. It was a desperate attempt when all else had failed. And it worked. He thrived, he said, for the first time in a long time. Meeting Ruby and having you on the way, Roman, changed him, too. He gained weight and became productive at school and the hospital.

"Soon after Ruby's death, he lost any health he had gained. It was so hard watching another loved one deteriorate and feeling helpless to do anything about it. Within a few weeks of Ruby's funeral, he took his own life by overdosing on pills."

Helen broke down again. Roman spoke. "This is so hard for you to relive. We all need to take time. Would you be OK if Ainsleigh and I get some tea and scones and bring them back?"

"Yes, dear. Of course."

He and Ainsleigh went to the nearby dining area of the complex and ordered tea and scones. They returned to Helen's apartment and choked down the refreshments as best they could. It seemed as though more tears were choked back than food or beverages consumed.

"I'm really OK, loves," Helen said. "Even though the hardest part of the story may be yet to come." She paused a bit and took another deep breath, which seemed to nourish not only her body but her emotions as well.

"As Ruby's health was getting worse and worse, I had some time to consider the possibility of raising Roman," Helen said. "At that point, I anticipated Lewis could help. I'm not sure what would have happened if Lewis had lived, but I made the hasty—but informed, I thought—decision right after his death that you deserved better than a middle-aged woman, already worn out from medical trauma and tragedy, to raise you. And I was honest with myself. I knew my decision was as much about me as for you. But I've always been a believer in adoption—even if it was only from a philosophical point of view. Of all the difficult things I've endured, including burying my daughter and son-in-law, giving you up probably was the worst."

She told Roman how the adoption occurred—through the hospital chaplain who knew of a couple in a neighboring town who already had an adopted daughter. Helen signed all the documents so Roman could stay in touch. When she didn't hear anything from or about him, she assumed the worst. Having lived through the trauma of a congenital lung disease with her daughter all of those years, she was convinced Roman had a more serious case than first suspected and hadn't lived.

Roman asked why she hadn't petitioned the court to find

out about him, and Helen said she didn't know that was allowed.

The sadness in the story was almost unbearable. But it didn't stop Roman from being Roman. He had found his grandma, and she seemed like a wonderful woman. And he had seen images of his mom and dad, and they had been loving parents whose opportunities in life were far more restricted than his. Yes, there was abject sadness in the loss, he knew, but Roman also knew he needed to focus on the joy inherent in what he, Helen, and Ainsleigh had.

"I think you both need to rest," Roman said. "Could we come back again tomorrow?"

"Oh, yes. Please do. If you don't mind, we can drive to the home where we lived when your mother was born. And I would love to see pictures of you growing up, Roman. I want to see your adoptive parents and your sister. Did you bring pictures of your wedding and your home in Arizona?"

"Yes. I have many of them on my phone. But you can see the most recent ones best on my laptop. And the older pictures are with us as well. In the excitement, I left them at the inn."

Neither Roman nor Ainsleigh were in the mood for eating out that evening. They ordered pizza from room service early in the evening. Thankfully, Ainsleigh fell asleep soon after they ate. She slept through the night.

* * * * *

They spent the next day with Helen. They orchestrated the day to make it as typical as it could be for a man and wife to spend time with his grandmother. It wasn't difficult at all. In fact, it was splendid. They took her for a ride, and she showed them significant places from her past. They all enjoyed the snow-covered journey. There were areas where the trees bowed over the roads and created a billowy white tunnel.

Helen loved the pictures of Roman, his adoptive parents, and Cori. He shared a good deal about Cori. Then there were the wedding pictures. Roman and Ainsleigh could tell this was a special time for Helen, and they promised they would put together an album for her as soon as they could.

"We need to get you on social media so we can share pictures with you immediately," Roman said. "Do you travel? Would you be able to come to Arizona?"

"Oh, yes! The van can take me to the airport. Tell me when to come, and I'll try. I've never traveled, so you'll have to tell me what I need to do."

The time came for Roman and Ainsleigh to leave. There still were questions that Roman needed to ask, and he wasn't sure whether Helen had purposely overlooked them or not. By then, however, he was calling her Grandma Helen.

"Grandma Helen, what about my dad, Lewis's, parents?"

Helen sighed. "I don't know," she began. "The pastor from his church and the hospital chaplain made all the arrangements following his death. There was no funeral. If his parents exist, they never have surfaced."

Roman and Ainsleigh tried not to be obvious as they exchanged glances. He couldn't be sure what she was thinking, but he was thinking his quest wasn't quite over.

Helen spoke again. "Please give Cori a special message of thanks from me. She must be a very special girl."

"I will. And she is." That gave Roman an idea. He snapped a picture of Helen and Ainsleigh with his phone and texted it to Cori on the spot. He added the message: "Gram Helen says thanks."

CHAPTER 20

FROSTED

"Della, I hate to tell you this, but you are almost totally covered in frosting!" Cori said with a laugh. "You obviously gravitate toward icy blue. And I think we have decorated about four times the number of cookies we possibly could devour for the entire season!"

They used all of the cookie cutters numerous times. As such, they produced stars, snowmen, Santas, Christmas trees, bells, stockings, and wreaths.

Cori was finding out more and more about Della and her seemingly indomitable spirit. "Hey, Cori, let's make special packages of cookies for people in your building. We can give them a wordless book, too," Della said.

"That's a great idea, Della. But they won't know what the wordless book means."

"We'll tell them if they ask, won't we?"

"OK. I can pick up the supplies after I drive you home. We'll make sure your mom is down with this latest idea too, OK?" Reina was, as Cori found out with a quick text exchange.

Cori drove Della home, picked up what she needed from the bookstore before it closed, and went to the grocery. She ran into an acquaintance who had been part of her study group when they were preparing for their master's degree comprehensive exam.

"Cori. Hi! How have you been?"

"Hey, Louise. I'm good. Sorry if I didn't see you at first. I was a little focused on a Christmas project I'm working on with a little friend."

"Who isn't distracted these days? Life just keeps getting busier and busier. Anything new in your life?"

Cori wasn't sure why Louise offered that question, but there it was! "Well, I'm looking for a new church. Any suggestions? I remember the lively discussions about theology that got us sidetracked from studying for our comps! I figure you should be a good source."

"Well, matter of fact, I've been volunteering at the local recovery program, The Landing," Louise said. "That's short for The Landing at Laurel Ledge. They also have a service on Sunday mornings. People in the dorms attend, as well as folks from the community. They're in transition right now while they look for a new executive director, but it's all pretty well put together. I like the service."

"Oh."

"They could use your help, too. Have you ever thought of volunteering?"

Cori gave a slight shrug. "Not until now. I might look into it."

"Oops," Louise said. "I have to run. I'm getting my hair cut in fifteen minutes."

"Well, good to see you, Louise. Thanks for the suggestion.

I'm thinking it's really good timing."

Cori couldn't get this encounter completely from her mind, and she contemplated what it might mean as she readied the project she and Della had planned for after school the next day. Roman and Ainsleigh were on her mind as well as she had her devotional time before bed. So much was rattling around in her brain, but she decided to focus on Della for the time being. Her PE teacher in high school said, "Do one thing at a time and do it well." She often needed to remind herself of that adage.

Cori spent some time in the office the following morning. There were always telephones to staff and emails that needed responses. She didn't have to be home until Della's bus arrived.

She had only been home for a short time when a neighbor brought by some mail that had been left in her box by mistake. She spied all the frosted cookie masterpieces. "Hey, Cori, have you started a bakery or something?" the neighbor said. "It's a great idea. You could call it Cori's Confections!"

"Thanks, Mrs. B., for the mail—and the humor! We'll make sure you get some—no charge!"

Della's mom had texted while Cori was still running her errands the day before. Reina had asked whether they could bring another girl to help, and Cori agreed if there was permission of the girl's mom, of course. So Cori was anticipating two special friends to help her.

A bit later, Della and her friend arrived. The kitchen once again looked disastrous by the time they were ready for their deliveries around the complex. It all went much more quickly than Cori envisioned, and was slowed only by the love of joke telling by Della and her friend, Margeaux.

"What do you call a melted snowman?" Della said, kicking it off. "Water!" she said with a laugh, providing her own answer.

"What's the difference between the regular alphabet and the Christmas alphabet?" Margeaux asked, determined to top the previous joke. "Noel!" she exclaimed.

They managed to finish the decorating and deliveries by dinnertime. They found some of the residents at home, and all were very thankful and cordial. To Cori's chagrin, Mr. Davis in the condo below her thought, of all things, that the girls needed a good Christmas joke.

"Hey girls, what does Santa use to clean his sleigh?" He left a very long pause before declaring, "Comet!" The girls covered their mouths and giggled. Cori was relieved the girls didn't seem provoked into more joke telling.

Cori texted the moms to ask if their girls could go out for a pizza, and both said yes.

"Hey, Cori. This is fun! I've never been on a G-N-O before!" Margeaux said, reciting the letters slowly as though to make sure everyone got an understanding of the acronym. Della said, "Yeah. It's what besties do, right Cori?" The rest of the incessant chatter was no less silly, but it was no matter. They didn't seem to disturb folks around them, and they were a pure delight to Cori.

After delivering the girls home, Cori practically fell into bed.

* * * * *

She didn't know what time to expect Roman and Ainsleigh the next day, so she went on with her schedule. Aware of how quickly the Christmas season passes, she decided to do some power shopping. She was pleased at how many excellent finds there were and returned home tired but pleased with her haul.

While she was shopping, Roman called and told Cori he wanted to get Ainsleigh home to Arizona, and resting, as soon as possible. "I am so torn because I want to come and tell you everything, but I promise we'll get to it eventually," he said. "Ainsleigh needs to get home. We've changed our airline tickets to depart from Albany, and we can turn in the rental car there. Please consider coming to Arizona for Christmas. Preferably an early Christmas!" Roman was really animated, even insistent. "It would be much better for Ainsleigh and so much fun for all of us!"

"Oh, playing the Ainsleigh card, huh? I guess I had better give it serious consideration, then!" Cori said. "Bye, Bro. Safe trip. Love you."

She had been thinking about their conversation ever since. Christmas in Arizona. She was so selfish not to have thought of it rather than thinking they should always travel to her. She would seriously consider it now.

The only highlight of the weekend other than preparing for work on Monday was attending the service at The Landing. There was a band, singers, and a full half hour of hymns, contemporary songs, and Christmas carols. There was a guest speaker who spoke only for a half hour, and then everyone was dismissed. It wasn't particularly polished, but everyone seemed so genuine. There probably were a little more than one hundred people in attendance. Cori found Louise's information accurate. Some in attendance were residents of the recovery wing, some were staff and volunteers, and the rest were from the neighborhood. It was mentioned in the bulletin that The Landing was in the process of hiring a new executive director.

After the service, there was a volunteer table. Cori signed up for volunteer orientation on Thursday evening.

CHAPTER 21

OLD YEAR'S RESOLUTION!

One of the first things on Cori's list for Monday morning was to have a face-to-face with Claris to see if she had heard any news from the Stowe area.

Claris wasn't available when she called, so Cori left a message. She covered the email, phone bank, and general inquiries, as she usually did when not on a major assignment. The time went by quickly, and she was a bit startled when her landline rang in her tiny office. It was Claris.

"Hey, Cori. Good timing. I just had a report from up north that you're going to want to hear. And I need to get out of here. The coffee shop on the first floor won't be busy yet. Do you want to meet there?"

Claris arrived first and was seated with a coffee when Cori

arrived.

"Hey, girl. Good to see you. How have you been?" Claris asked.

"I'm good, Claris. It seems like forever since our Vermont romp."

"Yeah. About that. Something came out of left field. It's off record, but you know that. Anyway, you already knew that a grand jury investigation was under way, right?"

"Yes. I kind of got that they were forced to use material witness subpoenas based on the autopsy to get folks to talk."

"That's right. It was pretty clear to the coroner that Anderson's body had been tampered with. It could have been the police, or friends, or both."

"Wow. Emory must have had them where he wanted them."

"Well, that's just it." Claris was animated and leaned forward in her chair instead of raising her voice. She didn't want to lose track of their surroundings and tried to be as quiet as possible. "Even with the subpoenas, Emory was dealing with people pleading the fifth, or bringing lawyers who were supposed to be silent but raised objections, or parents asking for alternate dates, or worse yet, letting their kids default on appearances. Emory was about ready to ask for indictments on all of them for failure to appear!"

"Could he?" Cori asked.

"Probably it wouldn't have done a bit of good. Even the judge was cutting the potential witnesses a lot of slack."

"Wow. What would you have thought if you had a case like that?"

"What a pain. And . . . it's what we thrive on!" Claris said.

"So, do you think he was complicit too?"

"I doubt that he was in on it. Just too stupid to realize the risks of what was going on. Do-gooder. Thinking he was doing the right thing."

"So, it really was going on? Is that what you're saying?" Cori was referring to the dangerous, self-indulgent practices she suspected of Anderson and likely others on the ski tem.

Claris slowed way down and punctuated each word of her response. "So it seems! Here's how it went down. The interscholastic sports association, of which the school was a part, got wind of the ski team preparing for the season before they were authorized to do so. That prompted an investigation, which led to them finding out about the grand jury inquiry slash obfuscation. That made them want to tighten the screws on the team in the worst way, and they threatened to make them ineligible for the season unless the whole mess was clarified pronto!"

"What? An ADA is helpless to get anything done, but the governing board of a sports association can?"

"You got it. Emory is just about finished questioning folks. It's beginning to become apparent that most members of the team were not involved, but almost all of them knew about it. They participated in the cover-up—including solidarity in wearing turtlenecks for the school pictures and keeping mum—just to avoid any scrutiny of the team. But when the tide turned and it looked like the season was in jeopardy, they had no interest in staying quiet, or worse—covering up the truth any longer. Sitting out the ski season was not going to happen for many reasons, not the least of which involved recruiting for colleges.

"It's going to take some time to determine the fallout, but child services already had made their determination and imposed the maximum fines on the police chief and athletic director for failure to report, though I think that's the least of their problems."

Claris continued without taking much of a breath.

"They both have been suspended from their jobs without pay. Emory thinks there will be criminal charges, but in saying that he was getting a little ahead of himself, in my opinion. But he done good. I won't take that away from him."

"What about the students?"

"Even less clear. He's thinking court diversion for mandated therapy would be leveled on any of the kids who were involved peripherally. Impeding an investigation would likely be the charge for the ones who were at the scene with the AD. Any involved in staging the scene after the fact could receive more than diversion. Emory doesn't think anything could have been done for Anderson to have prevented his death except not to have been involved in the risky behavior at all. But that might be wishful thinking. I think it's hard for any of them to think that anyone was there when it happened and could have summoned help in time. Even though folks are talking, there still could be elements of the story they are leaving out. I really hope none of these characters are that heinous."

Claris wasn't finished. "Oh, and you know what? Our tires were slashed by a student. Some guy named John. Apparently he wanted to keep us on the hook for solving the case without saying anything directly. He wasn't involved with the other students at all."

Cori knew just who that was. *Good for him,* she thought. She looked down and smiled for a brief moment. Then she raised her head.

"Is Emory going to keep you informed?"

"Emory has no obligation to keep us informed, but he told me he would do his best. He's afraid eventually it'll be all over the news. But it's unlikely that further testimony from you will be needed. Yay!"

Given the sordid situation, Cori felt guilty to feel . . . euphoric. But she was. She simply sat and stared ahead for a full minute. Inwardly, she was praising the Lord. Then, she did so outwardly! Finally, she looked at Claris and said, "Claris, I don't know how to thank you. You did this!"

"I don't know what to say. It's been a lot of work, I'll admit that. If all of the pieces and players hadn't fallen into place as they did, none of it would have come about. But Cori, you got everything started and gave us all the momentum to continue. Thanks for hanging in there."

Cori jerked her head toward Claris. She had another thought. "Trent. He was great too! Does he know?"

"He's about to, and it's going to cost him a dinner!"

CHAPTER 22

PRIVILEGED INFORMATION

Eventually, Cori asked if she could shift the subject.

"Shift? Exactly what does that mean?" Claris was a bit amused, but she was skeptical since she had no time to recover from her last caper with Cori.

"It's not an exact change of subject, since we first thought it might be related to this topic."

"OK. Spill it!"

Cori sighed quickly, but deeply. She needed a full breath before getting into this subject.

"Remember when Stewart seduced me, and I thought it was related to discrediting me with the church?"

"Yeah. Do you know more about it?"

"The big picture, yes. I'm going to avoid names to protect both of us from . . . whatever." As an aside, Cori uttered, "Wow.

This legal stuff has lost its luster for me!"

She continued. "Recently I befriended a little girl and her mom. Her mom, Reina, used to be part of the community about a decade ago. Reina arrived battered at a local pregnancy shelter, subsequently lost the baby at a hospital, and returned to the shelter to live for several weeks. She mysteriously disappeared after symptoms of a subsequent pregnancy became apparent. Before disappearing, she had shut down abruptly and stopped pursuing any kind of a life, preferring to stay locked in her room.

"Rumor was that she was whisked off to hide the fact that a prominent physician had fathered her child.

"Someone I know recognized her from the days she was at Compass Points and told me the story. She was shocked to see her back in the area and hoped I would keep a close watch out for her. I finally came to believe that's why I'm being targeted—because of my relationship with her."

Claris looked confused. Cori realized it sounded incredible, the way she had provided the facts.

"I'd better explain the connection," Cori continued. "The attacks on my character are coming from an individual who used to be my friend. She has a reputation among a few as a people user, and she has ambitions the physician's family possibly can deliver for her."

Claris still looked doubtful.

"Though I would love for you to believe me, Claris, what I need most is to know if anything can be done to protect my friend and her mother? I'm afraid for them."

"I so want to understand, Cori. I think it's OK to name names in this case."

"Dr. Dallas, Lourdes Dallas, my former friend Simone. The people for whom I am concerned are Della and Reina Carbone."

"I know, as an attorney, the names shouldn't have made a

difference. But they do. I understand. This is complicated. If it is exactly as you imagine, it definitely is an ethics violation, at the least. It likely could have been criminal if the pregnancy was forced, but the statute of limitations is only five years in this state. However, I know you didn't ask about that; you're concerned about their protection." Claris delayed a bit before continuing.

"You're a piece of work, Cori." Claris wasn't serious; she only was feeling a bit helpless. "Can you give me some time to think about this?"

"Sure. Sure. By the way, have you seen Stewart? Were you able to follow up on his false advances in any way?"

"Some. I asked security about him again after I heard about the would-be seduction. They've hired him before." She paused, then added, "They're not going to again. But he had been hanging around that day you first came to see me. He was chatting up Henry when I called for someone to travel with us. I think he followed you here and took a chance you were involved in the reason I needed security. Or maybe his hanging around Henry was part of a routine that finally paid off. Did anyone know about the Stowe-area case?"

"I don't think so," Cori said. "But I'll think on it. I wonder if he'll try anything again."

"You haven't noticed anyone lurking in the background, have you?"

"Once again, I don't think so. Thanks again, Claris."

Claris got back with Cori later in the day. "Hi, Cori. For the time being, I'm going to hire a private investigator to watch out for the Carbones, and also to investigate the relationship between Stewart and Simone."

"Great idea. I'll help pay for it."

"We can talk about that another time. For now, I can justify it until the Stowe-area case is disposed of."

Cori felt immediate relief. A PI should notice if anyone was observing Della or her mom. And she would be delighted to find out about Stewart. A PI investigating a PI! She couldn't help but chuckle. And if Stewart was worth his salt, he would notice he was being observed. That was even better!

She texted Roman and then sent nearly the same message to Byron. "Lots of progress on the Stowe-area case. Call." Both did within the hour. She gave them each the cliffs notes.

＊ ＊ ＊ ＊ ＊

The week was flying by. Cori heard from Roman every day and saw Byron frequently at work. They even collaborated from time to time on a report required for end-of-the-year statistical data.

Cori expected Della and possibly her friend on Thursday afternoon. A text from Della's mom alerted Cori to the fact that a couple more of Della's friends planned to come. Cori texted back: "The more the merrier as long as the parents write out permission since I'll be transporting them!"

Della and her entourage arrived right on time—due mostly to the promptness of the school bus that dropped them off. They were all girls, and Cori thought that probably was a good thing. Della was so anxious to tell the other girls about the wordless book. Luckily, Cori had a number of them left over from their cookie caper, and she always had enough beads to make the bracelets.

Della did such a good job of representing the colors of the book and the messages associated with each. Cori could tell that Della not only had been practicing, but probably doing so with these girls! Cori was needed for very little of the presentation. Afterward, two of the girls wanted to pray the prayer of faith. Cori began hatching a plan for Della to present the wordless book at a gathering in the common room of Cori's complex. It could be for folks who were curious about the book they had been given with the cookies.

All the girls were thrilled with Cori's condo. Della led the charge and displayed the bedrooms, turned on the Christmas decorations, and even showed them the cabinets where the supplies for cookie making were stored. "Oh. We want to cook too!" Janney said. This little girl was the most enthusiastic youngster Cori ever had met. She wanted to be in on everything.

"Next time you come, we'll have a pizzarette night," Cori said. "All of us can cook." Cori saw several of them wrinkle their noses. Janney and Louise said, almost simultaneously, "What's that?" She told them they would make mini pizzas out of English muffins, each adding the toppings of her choice.

The girls knew there wouldn't be pizza that night due to the session scheduled at The Landing that Cori had told them about. She chauffeured them home and went directly to the training.

Cori didn't expect such a bustling crowd at The Landing. She found out that not everyone was there for the training. There was a prayer group also set to begin. The search committee was gathering for an interview with a candidate for the executive director position. Everyone seemed to know where to go except for her, but she soon found out.

The training was fairly broad, but it was helpful for understanding some of the safety protocols for the building and center policies. She had a good thing going with Della and her group on Thursdays, so Cori steered away from Thursday responsibilities and volunteered to co-facilitate a group on Tuesdays. The fact that she had to travel for her job didn't bother the center. They were willing to be flexible.

* * * * *

Cori hadn't slept this well in a long time. She got up a little late on Friday. Work would occupy part of the day, but she dropped in on Ardis on her way.

The receptionist was as friendly as before—until she returned from announcing Cori's presence to Ardis. Clearly, the receptionist had taken on an air of discomfort, probably acquired from Ardis. "She might be able to see you if you wait. Better to make an appointment." Sensing she was unwelcome, Cori nearly left. But she sat down, telling herself she would give it a chance.

She was surprised when Ardis actually emerged. "Cori. Good morning. Come on in."

They both took a seat in Ardis's office. "Cori, I think I've gotten as far as I can with information on your adoption. Which is exactly nowhere." She paused for a moment. "I shouldn't even tell you this much, but the terms of your adoption stipulated that you never were to know about it. Your parents signed documents attesting and promising full confidentiality. I am so surprised there were any documents left in their files."

"Well, Roman admitted that the letter was all folded up in an old Bible of my mom's," Cori said. "The financial document was stuck to a larger, unrelated document. I'm sure they thought they had destroyed everything and simply overlooked these two pieces."

"I see."

"So, is a legal document null and void after the signers are deceased?"

"Not in this case. Everyone involved in the adoption could be deceased, and it still is to be sealed. This is very unusual."

"In your experience, what would be the circumstances warranting such secrecy?"

"That is impossible to say."

"Fear of a scandal?"

"No comment, Cori."

"I'll bet it is."

"Cori."

"I'm going to proceed on that assumption."

Silence.

Cori settled down a bit. She had to ask: "Could you be sued for giving even this amount of information?"

Ardis just gave her one of those *Really?* looks.

Cori gathered herself. "Well, I lived this long without knowing. I'll be OK. But this stuff has a way of biting folks in the butt. You can be sure that more people than the parties involved know about this. It could all come crashing down some day."

Silence from Ardis. And a smile.

"Thanks, Ardis. I really do appreciate all you have done. Let me fill you in on Roman."

And she did.

CHAPTER 23

DELIVERED

When Byron called off their next scheduled meeting due to the impending birth of his daughter, Cori immediately thought of spending the next few days in Arizona celebrating an early Christmas with Ainsleigh and Roman. Byron and Cori's report could and would have to wait. She would be sure to get it done by the end of the year. Roman jumped at the idea of her flying out, and she told him she would be on the next seat available after the baby arrived.

Cori was going to be ready to depart, and she whispered many prayers for the expected baby as she packed. She had concerns about being out of town, not the least of which was not seeing Della and her friends for the next ten days. She texted the moms about her plans so the young girls would know about her absence, and trusted Della's safety to prayer and the PI.

She hadn't forgotten about her commitment to The Landing and went by to let the leaders know she couldn't start this Tuesday. There appeared to be another session of the search committee just ending its work as she entered the building. She caught a glimpse of the candidate as he was leaving. Their eyes met, and she couldn't seem to look away. Nor could he.

There was a very good reason. This had happened before ... since this was her stranger! He was much taller than she and had very dark hair. He had an impressive presence, but struck her as humble and kind at the same time. For a moment, she thought he might come over and introduce himself. Her heart rate skyrocketed!

Someone pulled his attention away for the introduction of some folks who hadn't been part of the interview. Cori continued on, but each locked eyes once more before disappearing from one another's view.

Her heart continued racing. After all the arrangements she had made, she now wished—sort of—that she wasn't leaving town.

The phone call came as she was drafting a portion of the statistical report she and Byron had planned to complete as one of their tasks that day. Byron's little girl had arrived! All was well, and she weighed in at a whopping six pounds. Cori was relieved since the delivery seemed somewhat earlier than expected.

Cori got online and purchased a flight out first thing Saturday. She rushed out and bought a baby gift and had it wrapped, but when she went to pay for it, Cori realized she had skipped a step that was part of the routine whenever she traveled. Cash!

Cori didn't use ATM machines. She had given up using them at about the same time she stopped jogging. It wasn't her safety as much as it was a refusal to provide obvious opportunities for thieves and muggers. She remembered the branch of her bank that was open late on Fridays, and luckily it wasn't that far from the hospital.

She rushed inside the bank. Luckily, the lines weren't long. She checked the time on her phone, unaware of those surrounding her in line.

"Time to get a little cash for Christmas shopping?"

She was startled by one of the customers who had just finished a transaction and was on his way out.

"Stewart!"

"Hey. Ready for some more karaoke?"

Cori spoke as though she had rehearsed—but she hadn't. "Oh yeah, Stewart. This time, we could do 'Jar of Hearts.'"

"What?"

"Think about this and maybe it'll help you figure it out. I heard your part of the telephone call you made right after leaving me at my hotel door the last time I saw you. Good-bye, Stewart."

"Cori, let me explain."

"Oh yeah? Great! Because I want to hear everything about it. Believe me. But not now. I have a baby to meet and Christmas to celebrate. And they are both way more important than your vapid explanation. I know a lot more than you think I do. So you'd better use your penchant for fiction to make it good."

She knew it was a mini scene. Fortunately, it was her turn at the counter. She proceeded through her transaction, and Stewart had left by the time she was finished.

"For once, my impulsivity paid off," she whispered to herself. And she left for the hospital.

She hadn't a clue whether she would be able to see Byron, Cheri, and baby Elsa, but she was going to try.

She had no idea that the hospital's maternity wing was locked, but found out as soon as she arrived. After some back and forth over an intercom, she was allowed in. All of the nurses were in dull pink, and it struck Cori as comical. She wasn't sure why—the pink or the chuckle.

She found Byron, Cheri, and Elsa. Such contentment. The proud parents were so thrilled to show off Elsa. It was no wonder; she was sweet. Cheri's parents had just left, and there had been a number of other visitors already. Cheri was elated, for sure, but tired.

"I know you're tired, Cheri. I can't stay long. I'm going to take some time while Byron is on paternity leave. I'll be back on the Monday after Christmas."

Byron walked to the door of the room with Cori. Before saying good-bye, they looked back at Cheri, who, along with the baby, was dozing off. "Congratulations, Byron. They're perfect. Both of them!"

"Thanks for coming, Cori. Let us know as soon as you get back."

"Oh yeah. I will. Bye, Byron."

OK. So, how to get out of this place? Cori stood confused for only a split-second when a male—not dressed in dusty pink—smiled at her and said, "Can I help in some way?" She was embarrassed. "I have to confess I don't know how to get out of here." He was charming. "Here. I'll accompany you."

He was older, but very debonair. She guessed he was a doctor, but she wasn't sure. "Do you have a new little friend?"

"Oh, yes. And she's beautiful! This hospital obviously does good work!"

Cori was leaving when, of all people, she almost ran into Lourdes Dallas! Lourdes glared at Cori and, for a moment, Cori thought Lourdes might actually strike her. Then Lourdes glared at the doctor, who was in mid-sentence in greeting her when he slowed and looked at her questioningly. He obviously had noticed the open hostility toward Cori. As rattled as Cori was, at some point just before the door closed behind her, she noticed his name tag.

Dr. Rolland Dallas.

So that is Mr. Lourdes Dallas, Cori thought. With disdain. Life just kept getting more and more confusing. She didn't know whether to think the layers were unravelling or being wound ever tighter. She wished she could think of a way to protect women from that seeming monster in overtly dashing armor.

It had seemed like such a good plan to book an early flight. It made it easier for those on the other end who were picking her up at the airport, but now that it was bedtime, she really wondered if she would be able to wake up in time.

CHAPTER 24

DAWN

Cori slept. And well. But she awoke from her sound sleep and bolted upright in bed.

"Oh my lord! Lourdes!" She said it out loud. If there had been any spectators in her bedroom, they would have wondered about her sanity. She wondered about her sanity. It hit her in a moment. At least two people had mentioned Lourdes as the source of her problems. She suspected it was tied to Della. *What if it is about my own adoption? What if that is the secret?* "Oh, my word. What if it's both?" She said that aloud as well. Cori opened her mouth wide and dropped her jaw as far as it would go. "Oh no!"

She ran to her bathroom and wretched over the sink until she almost had no life left.

Could she pull herself together and get ready for her flight? Who could she talk with? Not Roman! Not Ardis! Jessalyn is probably at work! Simone! *Oh no. Where did that come from? There isn't anyone right now.* A thousand questions seemed to go through her mind. How would she arrive at the airport with enough lead time? How would she sit still on the plane? How could she live with these thoughts? "I have to do something," she said as she pulled herself together in her bathroom. "I have to at least get some answers. Maybe Della's mom can tell me something."

Cori postponed her flight until mid-afternoon. She texted Roman to let him know and apologized for how late it would be when she arrived. She assumed he would be asleep and wouldn't respond for an hour or so, but he got right back to her that he didn't mind the late flight. "What's up?"

Cori knew he would be curious. "I want to explain in person. OK?" Mr. Patience himself answered. "Sure."

It was still early when she ventured to contact Reina Carbone. She was being bold, but then, in what she considered a cowardly move, she chose to text. "I know I told you I was flying out this morning, but I really would like to talk to you before I go. Would you have any time this morning?"

Cori went through the motions of getting ready while waiting for Reina to get back to her. She wondered if she would get back to her at all, and whether finding out about Della's story would help her at all. Never mind whether Reina would be willing to tell her anything.

She heard the text signal from her phone as she was finishing her makeup. Cori grabbed her phone, cleared the screen, and clicked the text icon. It was Reina. "Sure Cori. Della is going to a friend's house while I'm at the market this morning. What do you have in mind?" Quickly, Cori texted back. "Lunch at the Sandwich Club? My treat, of course!" Right back came the message. "Yes. I can stretch my time away enough for a quick lunch. Noon?" Cori didn't hesitate. "Deal!"

Now she wondered what else she had gotten herself into.

How could she broach the subject with Reina? Was her impulsivity and curiosity going to cost her a relationship with Della? No doubt she needed to consider this further. As difficult as it was, she stopped the churning inside of her and spent some time in worship and prayer. She knew she needed direction before proceeding with what she had planned in the next few hours. It wasn't too late to stop the momentum.

"Heavenly Father, you made the world from nothing. Please make my praise worthy of you. Help me with all of my heart to thank you for life and salvation through your Son. Thank you for friends, safety, your Word, and the many provisions I enjoy each day. Please help me to accept your divine will and forgive me when I set up my own plans. Be my guide in the next few minutes, hours, and days. Help me to pursue your best for me and those in my world. Keep me from being part of the evil around me, and help me as I try to address the wrongs that have impacted the people I love. Help those who are acting out of self-interest to find you. Thank you. Amen."

Immediately, Cori felt ready to face the day, including her meeting with Reina and final preparations for her flight to Arizona. Her bags were packed and in the car so she could leave from lunch to the airport. She arrived at the Sandwich Club well in advance of Reina; the place was bustling with Christmas shoppers. The mood was festive, enhanced by the lush decorations and seasonal music. Space was at a premium, and Cori wondered whether they could find the needed privacy for the kind of conversation she envisioned.

It was interesting to Cori that this was one of the first times she was in the Sandwich Club without seeing someone she knew. She was glancing around the dining area to be sure she didn't recognize anyone when she noticed Reina enter. She gave a subtle wave, and Reina immediately noticed.

"How are you, Cori? I was so surprised to hear from you. I thought you would be on the plane to Arizona by now!" She gave Cori a huge hug as she spoke.

"I know. You'll understand in a moment. Let's get some food, and then we'll chat."

"That sounds good to me. I need some soup and a hot cup of coffee."

"Whatever flavor of coffee you get, be sure to try some of their cinnamon touch-up. It's great!"

"What else do you recommend? I don't eat out on a regular basis!"

"I love the pumpkin soup, if you like that sort of thing."

"Oh, I do!"

"Let's go!"

Both women ordered the same lunch, which was a bowl of "seasoned-all" pumpkin soup and gingerbread coffee with a cinnamon touch-up. Cori kept their table reserved with a pawn provided by the shop. As soon as they were seated, Cori spoke first.

"I don't want to keep you from home for long, so I'll get to the point," she said. Cori tried to be as gently honest as she could in her approach to the conversation. "I recently learned that I was adopted."

"Oh, Cori. That's huge. I'm sorry that I didn't know. What can I do to help?"

"That is so nice of you. I tried to find out about the adoption only to discover that all deals are off. No one is to know anything about the details—in fact, I was never supposed to have found out. There is a silver lining, though. We have always known that my brother was adopted, and through the process of going to court, he was able to find out about his family of origin. He actually met his grandmother recently. Sadly, his parents are deceased."

"Wow. That's a lot of information. You have been such a friend, and it's amazing how much you have been through that I knew nothing about. "

"You are being so kind. I feel a bit like a meanie for what I am about to ask you."

"Please. I'm a pretty tough broad. Go right ahead."

"A few weeks ago, when you and I were talking in the market, a friend of mine recognized you and told me she was surprised to see you back in Laurel Ledge—that you had lived here before. I didn't know that."

"Oh." Reina took a deep breath and paused a moment. She scowled slightly, but maintained her usual friendliness. "How did she say she knew me?"

"She had worked at Compass Points."

"I see."

"I know information on residents should be confidential. It's difficult to recount how the conversation unfolded, but she really cares about your best interest."

"I'm sure. And I know it was years ago. I don't mind telling you about it, Cori. But I don't know what it could do for you. Are you wondering if it is tied to your adoption somehow?"

"I don't know. I have a hunch. Sometimes my hunches have merit, but not always—for sure."

"Here's what happened," Reina began. "I was swept off my feet by a charming, handsome, important man who worked at the Dominican Embassy in New York—actually, the Dominican Republic consulate general. I needed the help of the state department on several occasions due to the immigration status of my parents, and I met him there. We hadn't known each other long when we decided to get married. What an amazing time we had dating. He spent a boatload of money on me and took me to the nicest places for dinner and shopping at stores I barely knew about. We married after knowing each other only a few weeks.

"All of his kindness stopped as soon as we were married. He was controlling and abusive. Because he worked for the state department, he had me convinced that nothing could be done because of his immunity from prosecution.

"I soon knew I was pregnant, and I didn't want my baby to face a life with him. I didn't want to either. I was scared to leave, but I was more afraid of what would happen if I stayed. I left in really bad shape and drove as far away as I could get. I found the pregnancy shelter, which happened to be in Laurel Ledge.

"I don't know how much you know about Compass Points, but they were superb in getting me medical care and making sure I was as safe as possible. I was so depressed when I lost my baby. I know without the help at Compass Points, I would have considered taking my life. Eventually I healed physically, but I knew I would only be really well if I put one foot in front of the other and started a new life. So I started hunting for a job.

"One day I had just left an interview at a dentist's office when my husband caught up with me. I don't know how he found me, but his car was nearby and he shoved me in before I knew what happened. We hadn't driven far when he pulled over and assaulted me, including, you know, intimately. Even though he had blindsided me, I knew it was stupid to think he never would find me. I always carried mace pepper spray with me. I even had a license to carry and had it in my hand most of the time when I was in public. I must have been too absorbed in afterthought about the interview and forgot to have it in my hand, but it was in my purse where I could grab it quickly.

"He was putting himself back together and getting ready to drive when I pulled out the mace and assaulted him with it. I smacked him in the head with my purse, which also had a brick in it. While he was stunned, I grabbed his arm and twisted it around the steering wheel. He was writhing from the pain of the mace and the attack. Probably what made it work was the surprise—I had never used any moves on him before that. I grabbed the keys out of the car and ran as fast and far as I could.

"I threw the keys into the tall grass of a nearby field as hard as I could and used my cell to call 911. It's a good thing cell phones give a location, because I didn't know where I was. I was running and screaming the whole time. I had no idea if someone could hear me. Someone did, because the police arrived quickly and took me to the hospital. They also took my statement and said my husband was being arrested. I was examined at the ER, and then they released me to Compass Points.

"By then, the police had backed off filing charges, but they did issue a stay-away order. Compass Points made arrangements for me to stay secluded, and they said they hired security. The people who worked security posed as volunteers, so I don't think hardly anyone at Compass Points knew about the attack or the extra protection. The doctor made all of the arrangements as far as I know.

"It seemed like only a few days when I realized I was pregnant with Della. Probably it was longer than that. It had been a few weeks when a lady I had never seen before came by and said funds had been donated for me to be relocated. I was shocked, but grateful, because I didn't know what else to do. Within hours, someone I had seen often at Compass Points helped me get my things together and drove me to a new location. I remember he was this strong, burly guy who seemed out of place there. But he was very professional in helping me to my new apartment. It was in Missouri. I had enough money to get settled and get by until I found a job. There was a bit of a nest egg left to help out for six weeks after Della was born and before I could return to work, and to help with daycare. I can't say enough about Compass Points."

Reina seemed to change her focus completely. She took Cori's hand and said, "Does that help with your questions about your adoption?"

Cori could hardly recover enough to answer. Reina's story was beyond anything she could have imagined, and so dissonant with her stupid hunches.

"Reina, I have always admired you and Della, but never so much as now that I know all you've overcome. You are amazing. Your story is amazing."

"Thank you, Cori. Thank you for introducing us to the Lord, who made us overcomers in it all."

Cori didn't immediately respond.

"So, did anything have a connection with what you were thinking about your own adoption?" Reina asked. "Are you comfortable telling me?"

Cori shook her head as if to bring herself back to reality. "Oh. Actually, no. Truthfully, I was suspecting some pretty foul activity coming from Compass Points, but your story has wrenched me from those thoughts for the time being."

"Do you think your family of origin is connected to Compass Points in some way?"

"Actually, not at the moment. I don't know what to think. I'm sorry to be so mysterious. I promise I will let you know as soon as I have better information. Any information, in fact." Cori then realized Reina's story was a bit incomplete.

"Do you mind telling me why you felt safe coming back to Laurel Ledge?"

"Oh. I forgot to finish. Della's dad died this past summer. There really was no reason for us to leave our lives in Missouri, but I always resented that I had to leave such a wonderful place because of him. So, we came back. I'm glad we did."

"I'm so glad you did too! It has been wonderful getting to know you!"

"Thank you, Cori. Is there anything else I can tell you that might help?"

"Do you know the names of anyone who helped you at Compass Points?"

"Not the woman. She was very professional and business-like. For someone who was doing such a kindness for me, she was very cold and distant. Almost as though she disliked me immediately. I thought I saw her again at The Gathering when I first arrived, but she disappeared so quickly. The man never told me his name that I can remember—but it was Stewart. Don't ask me how I know that." Reina paused, then changed subjects.

"Cori, are you still planning to travel for the holidays?"

Cori gasped. She couldn't believe Reina's last comment, nor how she had lost track of the time. "Oh no! My flight leaves in less than two hours. I'm sorry to be so rude, but I really have to run!"

"Of course. Have a good trip, dear. We'll talk more when you get back."

"Thank you so much. I hate to leave you so soon after hearing your amazing story."

"Go!"

"Bye!"

CHAPTER 25

THE INFORMANT

Again, Cori postponed her flight. Besides, she thought, what's wrong with flying on a Monday? The airline didn't even charge for this latest change. This was getting so ridiculous that even Roman would probably begin to lose patience with her.

She decided to come clean with him. "Roman, your fickle sister is postponing until Monday. I'll text my flight number and arrival time. Before you say anything, I'm sorry. I know I'm a pain. Here's what's up. I met with Reina, Della's mom. She told me a fantastic story about how Compass Points helped her resettle in another state after being battered by and escaping her husband, twice. She told me about losing her first baby after escaping to Compass Points. Later, her batterer found her and attacked again. That is how she became pregnant with Della. The reason I'm delaying another flight is that I have to talk to Stewart. He's the security guy who tried to seduce me and also the man who was hired to help Reina relocate all those years ago!"

"Wow. Just wow." There was a long pause. And then, "Cori, maybe you should just take a break and think about this. You don't know what you're getting into with this guy."

"I know, I know. But I have to. I saw him Friday at the bank. Do you believe it? I didn't give him a chance to say anything, but I got the impression he was going to apologize."

"Cori. Come on. I think you're rationalizing just a tad."

"OK. But I'm going to anyway, even if I can't rationalize meeting with him."

"Have you contacted him?"

"No. I don't even know how. But I will."

"Yes. I know you will. Be careful, please. Is there someone who could go with you?"

"I really don't want to involve anyone."

"Could you wait for me to come?"

"Thanks. No. Really, no!"

"What are the chances we'll see you Monday?"

"Wish I could promise."

"By Christmas?"

"Yes." She dropped the apologetic tone and became even more pumped. Now she was enthusiastically saying, "And guess what else? I think Lourdes was the woman who financed Reina's relocation!"

"Coincidence." He stated it as though he really believed it was—but only for a second, before realizing better. "Wait, does that mean something?"

"Roman, I don't know. Sorry for the tone. But if I can find out, I'm going to. I realize she's married to the doctor dude who treated Reina at Compass Points, but if they funded the relocation, why didn't he just give her the money? Why did her fancy face have to get involved?" She knew her attitude had dissolved into cattiness.

"You're scaring me more than a little."

"It's OK. I'll calm down."

"You know, Cori, there's nothing to show that this is any of your business given what you just found out from Reina."

"There's the Lourdes-Stewart-me connection!"

"Right, but that doesn't make me feel any better about your plans." He hesitated a moment. "I guess I can't stop you. Love you. Bye."

"Bye, Roman. Sorry that I'm so much work."

Oish. Now what was her move? If she was delaying her trip in order to be in contact with Stewart, she'd better get to it. Did she dare call the head of security at Amity on a Sunday? Even if so, would he give her Stewart's number? She had an idea.

She logged in to the Amity staff website and checked the staff numbers. She got calls at home. Why not Stan?

"Hi, Stan. Sorry to bother you on a weekend. It's important that I talk with the PI who accompanied Claris and me to Vermont several weeks ago. Do you have his number?"

"Ah, yeah. I'll text it to you . . . at this number?" He paused. "But I thought there was an issue with him."

"Well, I'm going to find out. Thanks! I'll let you know how it goes."

She hoped that wasn't too misleading.

Her phone buzzed and she checked her text. It was Stan. Good. She saved the number in her phone and then dialed.

"Stewart Investigations."

"Stewart, it's Cori Sellers. I need help with an investigation."

"Yah. Huh? And you're calling me?"

"You could say that. Trouble is, I need to see you right away."

"Can it wait until after football?"

"When is that? I'm not a fan."

"I'm not surprised. Couple of hours?"

"I guess."

"Where?"

"How about the food court at the mall?"

"With all the Christmas shoppers?"

"OK. Not a good idea. How about the burger bar near the hospital?"

"Sure. See ya."

"OK."

The meeting was all Cori could think about. What was she going to do with herself for the next two hours? She supposed she could watch the Patriots game; then at least she would know when it was over. She found they were practically killing the competition when she tuned in, so she began watching one of her Christmas movies. *Meet Me in St. Louis* was one of her favorites, and she could enjoy it whether distracted or not.

The movie wasn't finished when she left the apartment, but it was time to meet. Stewart already had arrived and was waiting in his car in the parking lot when she pulled up.

He got out of his car while she was parking and walked over to open her door. She still sensed he was acting somewhat contrite—or at least was not the same confident man she had met several weeks ago.

"Hi, Cori. How are you?"

"OK. I appreciate your meeting with me."

"Sure. Let's go get a seat and see what I can do for you."

Cori felt childish for not wanting to meet with Stewart at her favorite eating and meeting place. But the Sandwich Club was special to her, and she didn't want any memories of Stewart next time she had a meal or snack there. She was beginning to regret it and remembered why she didn't come by the burger bar very often. It was noisy and the tables were close. Cori had forgotten you had to wait to be seated, but she took advantage of this reality and asked if there was a table a bit quieter than the ones closest to the entrance.

They were led to a table that wasn't too close to the rest of the crowd, but still public enough that she was following Roman's demand that she stay safe.

The host left menus, and Stewart hesitated—to show he was going to follow her lead.

Finally, Cori said, "Do you want to order?"

"Yeah. I do. How about you?"

"I think I'll just have a hot chocolate."

They waited in silence until they had ordered their beverages.

Again, Stewart waited for Cori to say something.

Cori finally broke the ice. "Some game, huh?"

"Yeah. Not really competitive, but lots of scoring. You saw it?"

"Not really. I tuned in for a bit but tuned out when I saw the score."

Stewart chuckled a bit. Then waited again. When Cori said nothing, he finally spoke.

"Since I have the chance, I want to apologize for my behavior in Vermont."

"Actually, it wasn't your behavior, per se, that was offensive. It's why you did it. I don't think I can do anything with an apology until you've dissected the backstory for me."

"OK. I'm practically on retainer for a lawyer who asked me to try to seduce you."

"Lourdes Dallas."

Stewart's head jerked back and he stared at Cori. He scowled, but his expression soon changed to a crooked half smile. "How did you know that? If you ever give up your day job, you're hired."

"I suspected right away. That's part of the reason we're here, and there's more I want to ask you. Is there some PI/attorney privilege you're going to invoke?"

"Well, she's been a good source of dough for a long time,

but given what a jerk I was to take that job, I'll do the best I can."

"Did she hire you to take Reina to Missouri?

"Oh, geez." He hunched forward and his voice became measured but not threatening. He was blown away by her at that moment. "Are you kidding me? How did you know that?"

"I was told. I'm friends with Reina, and she told me her story for the first time just this afternoon. She mentioned a PI named Stewart. I had enough other information to put some of this together. But I still have some questions."

"Like what?"

Cori shifted and now jerked her head back. "Wait a minute. Why don't you tell me first why you agreed to try to seduce me?"

"I'm a jerk. I told you. And I'd done a lot of work for her since that first job with your friend Reina. I thought I'd just see what happened. When I took the job, I didn't know whether I would really follow through. I thought I'd check out the situation and take it from there. I know you don't care, but it became less a job and more something I really wanted."

"Jerk. Don't even try. I heard your part of the conversation when you called her."

Stewart rolled his eyes and his skin tone momentarily turned nearly white. He cursed. "I'm sorry. I called to get it over with. Reporting back to her, that is." He cursed again. "I was glad you turned me down. As much as I loved making out with you, I was glad I couldn't deliver on whatever it was she wanted out of the situation." He slammed his hands on the table in front of him, leaned back, looked to the left, shook his head, and again said, "Geez."

"Well, there's more. Do you have any idea what her involvement with Reina was?"

"I guess it's OK to tell you since she never said anything, really. But it was pretty clear to me that I was hired numerous times to check out her husband's alleged affairs. My guess is she thought he was spending a little too much time at Compass Points, and that Reina was the reason. She told me to act as though I was a security officer there, so I did. No one ever questioned my status. A little before Reina's relocation, rumors had started that she was pregnant. Reina kept to herself, so I had nothing to report to Lourdes, but I guess she thought her husband was responsible for the pregnancy."

"But he wasn't, Stewart. If you still have a way of letting Lourdes know that, please do! Reina's batterer, who also was her husband, hunted her down while she was job hunting one day and attacked and raped her. It wasn't Dr. Dallas. He really helped Reina. Didn't you notice Reina's bruises?"

"No. I didn't. I must have been hired a while after the attack."

They were silent for a long time.

Finally, Stewart spoke. "I get that there's a lot I don't know. Like, why you are involved?"

"I guess I was targeted by Lourdes because of my friendship with Reina, or primarily with her daughter Della. I think she would love it if Reina disappeared again. It would be great if you could tell her there's no need to harass me or Reina. By the way, Reina came back because her husband is dead. I can't believe you never asked her about her past. You could have cleared this up a long time ago."

"Thanks for making me feel so good about it."

"I'm not going to apologize."

"I am. Again. I am sorry for what I did and for my involvement in this mess."

"OK."

"Do you trust me?"

"Good grief, no!"

"What do I need to do?"

"Show me that you can be trusted. Tell Lourdes the truth."

"Done."

"I don't know why I'm telling you this, but this went beyond Lourdes hiring you. I think she enlisted the help of my best friend too. Former best friend, I should say. It cost me my ministry with the church and youth group too."

"I don't get the connection."

"My so-called best friend is ambitious. I suspect Lourdes can help with that. The former friend also was my supervisor at church."

"Cutthroat."

"Don't get me started."

"You might be better off without a friend like that."

"True, but that's rich coming from you. And right after you asked me to trust you!"

"I deserve that."

"I have to go. Make this right?"

"OK. I'll get back in touch soon. Uh, can I ask if anything came of the investigation in Vermont?"

"Oh, yeah. They're making some progress." She gave a brief explanation and left him sitting at the table.

Cori didn't feel like finishing her movie when she returned to her condo. Then it dawned on her that she should fill in Claris.

Cori had Claris's cell number from their travels to Vermont, so she texted to ask if this was a good time to chat. Claris called immediately.

"Hey, Cori! Are you a psychologist or a psychic?"

"What do you mean?"

"Once again, I was about to call you."

"Oh yeah? What about?"

"Uh-uh. You reached out first. What's up? Are you in Arizona, by the way?"

"No. I postponed my flight twice already. I had to have two meetings before I could go away and enjoy Christmas. One with Reina Carbone and one with Stewart the PI."

"Oh?"

"I asked Reina more about her story. Claris, it was incredible."

Cori proceeded to give her the summation, as it were, then told her that she had filled in Stewart as well.

"Amazing." It was all Claris could think to say. Some response, she thought to herself, for someone who is supposed to be a mouthpiece!

"So, I don't think we need to spend more money on a detail for Reina, nor surveillance of Stewart."

"Agreed. Did either of them mention that they had noticed?"

"No. I forgot about it with each of the meetings. But I still delight that, either way, whether Stewart noticed or not, it's amusing."

After a pause, Cori asked, "Now, do you have news?"

"Oh yes." Claris's tone changed completely. "It's possible it's even more shocking than your news."

"Yikes."

"Yeah. There is going to be an indictment coming out of Vermont, and it might just make the news down here. So, I wanted you to know about it ahead of time. He's a 'trust fund' loafer who hangs out at his parents' ski condo. Apparently, he's in between job losses and college semester failures and occupies himself by endless partying. He and Anderson hung out, and he's the source of information to Anderson about all sorts of high-risk activities. Anderson was with him the night he died. They both were involved in the behavior, and Anderson was in obvious trouble. Rather than call for medical assistance, said friend called one of Anderson's high school friends, who he knew from previous parties. I'm unclear on all of the details, but they relocated Anderson to his home and staged the apparent suicide.

"They called the one adult they thought they could trust, the coach. He immediately saw through the ruse since he had gotten wind of the range of partying going on. Coach called his brother, the chief. The chief was off duty and a good distance away, so he called dispatch for immediate response. But then he took over the case when he was able to get to the scene. But you already knew that.

"Before I forget to tell you, all of this would have been suppressed if we hadn't contacted the local DA's office. The regular coroner was away for the weekend when Anderson died. The preliminary report, which was offered as 'a straightforward suicide,' was going to be accepted as the final report. It was done by someone specially assigned by Chief Barrett. All of these adults thought they were protecting the kids. I wonder if it ever dawned on them that they were actually complicit in continuing the risk of harm.

"I'll get more details, but for now the plan is to charge 'trust fund' with negligent homicide. The adults and the student will be charged with interfering in a police investigation. The substitute coroner, chief, and the coach will lose their jobs. It's sad, but they'll have to retool and find another line of work.

"All the kids who initially lied while being deposed also will be charged, but if they cooperate with diversion, the charges will be dropped."

CHAPTER 26

VERY MERRY

Amazingly, Cori slept. Overslept. The drive to the airport was harried and hampered by heavy traffic. Once again, shoppers, she presumed. Assuming no time for shuttle parking, she parked in the nearest lot. This was going to cost her!

She cleared security and tried to settle in. But her mind kept racing. How could she have been so wrong about Reina and Compass Points? Compass Points had helped Reina. How could such a cacophony of words from so many result in such a mess? So many words; such a lack of communication. *The world is so upside down*, Cori thought. Was she just as wrong about her situation?

Cori decided to browse through the bookshelves at the variety counter, but she wasn't really paying attention to anything she saw. Then she remembered she had her own e-book. She bought a coffee and Danish, picked up some water, and sat down to read one of her Christmas novellas on her e-book. Her leg never stopped moving the whole time she waited. She let the coffee get cold, the Danish was uneaten, and she was on page twenty-five of the novella when she realized she had no idea of the plot. She sighed at least every fifteen seconds.

She glanced up to be sure of the time, even though the time was on her tablet. And then, everything froze. Her leg, the time, the pretend reading—all of it. She had seen *him*. Her stranger. He was here. The candidate from The Landing. He saw her, too. The stare was much better than a glance—and a little scary. "Act like a grownup," she whispered to herself. "This is the best thing to happen in a very long time." Rising from her seat, she started toward him and he toward her.

He spoke first. "Good afternoon. I'm sorry we weren't introduced the other day. I'm Micah Flores."

"Cori Sellers. It's good to meet you. Can I assume you were being interviewed for the executive director position at The Landing?"

"Uh, well, yeah. Actually, they offered me the job."

It was at that moment Cori's flight was called to begin boarding.

She barely heard the announcement. "Have you made a decision?"

"Yes. I told them yes. I look forward to starting soon. Are you involved with the mission as well?"

"I just completed the orientation and will begin after my Christmas visit with my brother."

Second call for boarding. Cori didn't hear—or care—and ignored it again.

He spoke again. "Where is your brother?"

"Phoenix."

"That's where I'm headed. It's home . . . though only for a few more days! I'll be moving to Laurel Ledge right after Christmas."

Transfixed. Cori was absolutely transfixed.

"So, that is my flight," Micah said. "Is it yours?"

"Oh! Yes!" Cori finally snapped out of it and recognized that things other than this conversation were taking place.

"What section are you?" Micah asked.

"B. B-14."

"I'll be in line with you, just a little farther back. Save me a seat?"

"Oh, yes! Yes, I will."

Her stranger was traveling with her for Christmas!